Those Left Behind

KAREN GREEN

UK BookPublishing.com

For *Mother*, who's never stopped believing in me even when I didn't believe in myself.

Design, typesetting and publishing by UK Book Publishing

www.ukbookpublishing.com

ISBN: 978-1-916572-80-5

Acknowledgements

First of all, a huge thanks to UK Book Publishing who have made this book possible. In particular, I'd like to thank Jay, for designing the most incredible cover and interior format. He has brought my little story to life and elevated it into something magical.

Of course, thanks also to my wonderful family who have supported me and helped me with decision-making in regards to this book. I'm eternally grateful to have you as my family and first proof-readers.

Last, but by no means least, thank you to everyone who's ever encouraged me to follow my dream. It's because of people like you telling me not to give up that I am here today. This book was written in a very difficult time.

Being autistic has not helped me in the outside world and I have found myself in writing short stories, and hopefully in becoming a good author with further books in the future.

I think this story reflects my dark place. It is a harsh, cruel world that almost destroys Ella, but a small hope, a single chink of light, keeps her going and we reach the happy ending. In many ways I identify with Ella because I once felt lost and lonely, but with time and healing I understood there's always a better future waiting for us, we need only to have the courage to find it. I hope you enjoyed reading it as much I did writing it, and thank you for choosing my story. It makes me very happy.

Karen

Before

Twenty-one years ago, human kind was on the verge of extinction. The Earth- our ancestral home- had been ravaged beyond recognition. Climate change had reached a point of no return and nature, once our friend and life source, had turned on us. Ceaseless greenhouse gas emissions had polluted the atmosphere and made it thicker. As a result, almost no sunlight could escape into space and the global temperature rose to unprecedented levels. Because we had destroyed so many of our forests in the name of industry, there were not enough trees to control the rampant carbon dioxide levels and a vicious chain reaction ensued.

Sweltering temperatures caused glaciers to rapidly melt. Thousands of tonnes of ice plummeted into the ocean and the added weight of water made the seas rise. They swallowed entire islands whole, flooding low-lying lands and changing the map irreparably. Many thousands of people were displaced, and they fled to neighbouring countries in the hope of sanctuary.

Their neighbours, however, were faring no better. Warming, deeper oceans led to intense tropical storms that flattened entire coastlines and caused untold economic damage. Droughts became more commonplace and lasted much longer, especially impacting poorer nations who had contributed very little towards climate change. Harvests failed as water became more and more scarce, resulting in global food shortages.

Nobody was safe. Rich world powers assumed money could fix anything, but this argument melted in the face of crippling wildfires that swept the places that had escaped everything else. Many millions died across the world because of all of these dangers, and people were really panicking. This was the apocalypse, raw and real and terrifying, and we didn't have a way out. We had neglected and abused the Earth for so long, and now it was doing the same to us.

Things were hopeless. Humanity was doomed…

One

S *ilence*

Ella stood in a corridor, alone. The basic strip lights overhead were turned off, but even in the dim gloom she saw that she was lost. It was a plain corridor, devoid of any decoration, absent even of doors. It turned at a 90 degree angle further ahead, and twisted out of sight. And still the silence remained, deafening in its loudness.

She was frightened, although what of, she couldn't say. The only sound was the thumping of her own heart, a dull metronome in the dark, a resounding drum march. She swallowed nervously, her throat dry; little beads of sweat dripped down her forehead despite the cold chill in the air. Unease filled every part of her being, nervous anticipation of something happening itching away at her until she wanted to scream.

She couldn't stay here. Cautiously, she started moving forward, each tentative footstep rebounding off the walls in an eerie echo. The walls themselves, she noted, were made of a familiar white stone, and running her hand along them, they felt cool and hard.

As she walked, she felt her breathing calming, the tension in her muscles relaxing. She had no idea what she was looking for, but knew with absolute clarity that she could only find it if she kept a level head.

"Ella."

The voice made her jump. She had supposed that she was completely alone. Turning to locate the source, she saw a person standing in the middle of the corridor. A strange light illuminated their features. It had no apparent source, as the ceiling lights were still off.

Ella recognised her mother immediately. All her fear melted away, so glad was she of her company. She quickly rushed to embrace her.

But this wasn't right. Her mother had passed away nine years ago.

Her mother did not smile, and looked at her daughter with a grave expression on her face. She spoke again, in a worried tone full of warning.

"Run, Ella," she instructed. "Leave here now. You are in terrible danger."

"I don't understand." None of this made any sense. What was going on? "Why am I in danger?"

Her mother shook her head. "I don't have time to explain it. Just run, darling. Get out of here now. Seek…"

Her words were cut off by a rumbling noise. Ella spun around, bewildered, but saw nothing. The corridor looked exactly the same.

"Mum, what's happening?"

No answer. Her mother was gone. In the blink of an eye, the space she had occupied a moment ago had become thin air.

"Mum?"

A louder groaning answered her call, promptly followed by a crashing sound. For a brief second, she stood confused. Then she started running, sprinting as fast as she could in a blind panic.

The concrete floor was collapsing. Entire chunks of it cascaded into a never-ending black abyss below, although the walls remained intact. She ran faster, faster, to escape it, but it kept pace with her. There was no logical reason for this to be occurring, and yet it seemed to *follow* her, determined to chase her down.

She squealed round the corner, and suddenly her heart lifted. There was a door! An open door right at the dead end, through which she noticed scenery she didn't recognise. It seemed to resemble the surface- a tall tree grew out of verdant green grass, and above that, a picturesque blue sky. She had only ever read about such things before.

Ella dashed towards it, but suddenly the floor sped up. It was at her heels- she tried desperately to reach the door, to go through it, but the floor was giving way beneath her- she was falling, weightlessly, down into the chasm...

"NO!"

She opened her eyes. She was in her bed. Just a nightmare. She flopped back down onto her back and stared at the ceiling, her heart beating out of her chest.

The room was dark, because the light was off. It was the same simple strip light as in her dream, but she didn't need it to know what the room looked like. It was a small square, made of the same white stone walls and concrete floor. A faint blue glow was visible from the analogue wall clock, on the wall opposite her bed, above the door. It told Ella that the time was currently ten minutes past midnight. By the clock's gentle hue, the shadow of the wardrobe and desk in the corner was just noticeable. In the farthest corner, to the north-east, Ella knew there was a tall shelving unit, and in the middle of the room, just beyond her reach, was a circular table surrounded by four chairs. The door to the bathroom was out of sight, along the back wall.

This room was as familiar to her as anything could be. And yet, the sight of it now made her slightly sad, for some inexplicable reason. Perhaps it was the uniformity of it all; the fact that she knew everyone in Sector Four had the exact same furniture in the exact same layout in the exact same standard white and green colouration. No individuality. No personality. It was all emotionless.

Or maybe it was the memory of her mother troubling her. It had been disconcerting to see her dead mother, and it had been made worse by her ominous message. *Run, Ella. Leave here now. You are in terrible danger.* It could, of course, refer to the collapsing floor. But Ella sensed there was more to it than that. Some deeper meaning she had yet to unpick.

Ella had been born here, in this great concrete bunker. Her mother had come here when it opened twenty-one years ago, six months pregnant with Ella. She had been hoping for a better chance in life for her child, and followed most of what remained

7

of humanity down here. But she didn't truly belong here; she longed to return to the surface one day. She told Ella stories about it, back when she herself was a girl and it was safe to be there.

"It was so beautiful," she told a young Ella, who was listening eagerly as only little children can. "There was a forest just outside the city. All you could see was rows of towering green trees, and beyond that was a small river. We used to swim in it in the summer, and when the sun rose the light sparkled like diamonds on the water."

Ella's mother missed the surface greatly, and compensated by teaching her daughter all about it. Ella was more knowledgeable than most her age about the surface world. But nobody dared go there now. You were told too many horror stories by your parents to do that. Everyone knew it was dangerous. The thunderstorms, the toxic polluted atmosphere, the hostile locals who had stayed behind. The Thickair.

A noise in the distance startled her out of her thoughts. It was late. She had to get back to sleep, she had work tomorrow. She lay in silence, staring into space, until eventually, sometime after one o'clock, she dozed off, her last thought before she gave into the blackness at the edge of her vision of her mother.

Two

The sound of the alarm was what woke Ella up the next morning. Eight o'clock- the wake-up. Groaning, she begrudgingly sat up, stretching and yawning, trying to shake off the last remnants of her deep slumber. Ella had never been a morning person, and even after twenty years still found the morning wake-up difficult.

As she dragged herself to the wardrobe in the corner, her legs heavy with fatigue, to change into her work clothes, she heard the speaker click. A moment later, a voice began to speak, as loud as if they were in the room next to Ella. It was a woman's, light and airy, almost ethereal. She recognised it immediately as belonging to Megan Masters, the recently elected new Leader.

"Good morning, everybody," she said chirpily, in a sing-song tone. She reminded Ella of one of those fairy-tale princesses, incessantly cheery and just, always saying how much she wanted to help others. Ella had never liked her. "Let's get on with the morning announcements, then, shall we? It's Friday the 17th of June, and I have some bulletins here to share with you all. First, the breakfast special today is pancakes. Sounds delicious to me. Please enquire at the service window if you're interested. Secondly, today is your last chance to get tickets to tomorrow's children's craft day, taking place from 12pm to 4pm in the communal area. Only ticketholders will be allowed in from midday, so be sure to ask at the desk in the communal area. It's sure to be a fun family event!"

Ella done her best to ignore Megan as she got dressed, pulling on her work top and tying her shoelaces. Her uniform consisted of a plain white buttoned blouse, with a simple black jacket over the top and unremarkable black trousers. Her curly jet black hair cascaded down below her shoulders, covering up her plastic name tag. As she grabbed her bag off the central table and headed for the door, having just exited the small bathroom, she heard Megan finishing the morning announcements.

"And last, but not least, a very happy birthday to Martha Goodman, courtesy of your husband Jason.

Have a wonderful day!" Megan paused for a second, and then carried on. "Well, I think that's all from me today. I hope you all have an excellent day, whatever you're doing!" The speaker clicked again, signalling the announcements were finally over. Ella barely paid any attention to it as she pushed open the door and walked into the corridor beyond. Other people were emerging from their rooms, too, bleary-eyed and tired-looking. Each room had the same dark grey metal door, the only embellishment a gold number and a keypad. Ella's room was labelled number 503.

The door locked shut behind her as she left. The corridor into which she walked looked almost identical to the one in her dream, the same strip lights, white stone walls and concrete floor. The only difference was that everywhere she looked there was either a door with a person walking through it, or an e-poster. An e-poster was basically a screen attached to the wall, with various designs depicted on them. One showed just a few words, emblazoned in yellow against a grey brick background: TRUST, DEMOCRACY, FRIENDSHIP and HARD WORK. These were the Underground's founding principles, and each and every person here was meant to embody them. From a young age, children were taught these four ideals so that they would become good citizens of the Underground, and do their jobs without complaint. The only reason this place had survived twenty-one years was these values, encouraging everyone to work hard for the greater good and keep things running.

Another e-poster further down the corridor showed a young woman, a tall brunette with long straight hair and a complexion the colour of freshly laid snow. Bright green eyes shone out of her pale face, contrasting with the blue suit she wore; she stood with her arms crossed, leaning backwards so that her back touched the edge of the screen. Large letters beside her photo screamed the words 'MEGAN MASTERS: YOUR NEW LEADER'. She even *looked* like a princess, or so Ella thought when she noted the snowy face, the friendly gleam in the eyes and the beaming smile that seemed to suggest that she was approachable and kind. Ella had never been sure why she didn't like her- Megan was probably a perfectly nice and competent person. She was just too idealistic, too eager to please, too goody-goody. She was too perfect.

She tried to put Megan out of her mind as she proceeded down the corridor. The Underground was very large; she remembered getting lost the first time she tried to navigate her way out of Sector Four, when she first moved there. Now, though, she knew the way like the back of her hand, and promptly she was out of Sector Four and walking down the main corridor that connected all the Sectors, towards the cafeteria.

It was busy this morning.

The cafeteria was one massive room, with a large kitchen in the far corner. Where she stood, she was surrounded by tables and chairs as far as the eye could see, each filled with somebody eating their breakfast. There were probably around three hundred people alone eating at a table, the gentle hubbub of many conversations like a buzzing in the air. There were screens on the walls here, too, rectangular ones with menus on. Ella remembered that the special today was pancakes – that was probably why there was an enormously long queue at the service window. Ella didn't particularly fancy any of the pastries or breakfast cereals available from the self-service counter, so she supposed she would have to go to the back of the queue and hope it cleared quickly.

Just as she was about to do so, however, someone called out her name.

"Ella! Over here!"

She turned to look for the source, and smiled when she realised it was Nathan, waving her over from a nearby table. She quickly walked over and took a seat next to him. It was then that she noticed there were two lots of breakfast on the table: his favourite, jam with toast and a flat white, and her favourite, bacon and eggs.

"I saw that it was busy today, so I got yours as well," Nathan explained.

"Thank you so much, Nathan," she gushed, taking a bite of the bacon. "I can't describe how much I needed this."

Nathan looked well this morning. He had a cheerful smile on his face and looked energetic and ready to face the day. He had messy red hair and a freckled complexion, and big round brown glasses that made him look like an owl. He wore jeans and a red plaid shirt, one of his favourite outfits.

Ella and Nathan had been childhood best friends. They were in the same year in school, and Nathan was very intelligent, very good with computers. As a result, he was often bullied. One day, Ella caught some bullies tormenting him and stepped in, and they'd been firm friends ever since. Nathan often said that he was glad to have somebody who understood him and would listen when he talked about hard drives and RAM. Ella often said that she was grateful for a single friend at a time when she felt incredibly lonely and really needed someone other than her mother to talk to.

Of course, she still felt lonely to this day. But she'd gotten used to the feeling, so it didn't bother her anymore.

"That's no problem," Nathan was saying now, jolting her out of her daze. "I enjoy doing things for you, my lady."

That was their little in-joke. Ella had once commented that Nathan was very civilised and polite, never wanting to offend anyone. She had called him a gentleman, and so, in return, he started calling her 'my lady'. She hated it and he knew it, but that was what so special about having a friend like Nathan. He got her, and no-one else did.

"I am not a lady, sir," she retorted, laughing despite trying to be serious. She couldn't help it. Nathan just made her laugh. In fact, his presence made this whole place seem less oppressive and cold.

And in that moment, she realised that life wasn't so bad.

Three

After breakfast with Nathan, Ella said goodbye and headed to work. She worked as a librarian in the library in-between the communal area and leisure centre. It wasn't the most exciting job in the world, but she enjoyed it because of the peace and quiet.

Today she was helping her colleague Katie at the checkout desk. This was generally quite an uneventful task, as not many people came into the library at all, so after helping a few students take out some books for their studies, they got to talking.

Apparently Katie's young son, Sam, had just got an A in his Maths exam and Katie was brimming with pride.

"He's really struggled with Maths before. I'm so glad the one to one tutoring is working."

Ella was glad to hear this. As she herself had nothing interesting to contribute to the conversation, she and Katie just talked about generic things like their colleague Jessica's recent engagement, until suddenly Katie said something unusual.

"Do you ever think there's more to life than just this?"

This threw Ella a bit, as she had never heard Katie say anything like that before. She wasn't sure how to respond, so simply said, "What do you mean?"

Katie sighed. "I don't know. It's just- Sam asked me the other day if there was anything more to life than we have now, and I didn't know what to say. I mean, what do you tell a seven-year-old when they ask you that? And then I got to thinking, well maybe he has a point. I mean, think about it. We all do the same things every day- get up at eight as we're told, go to work, go to sleep in our identical beds, and repeat the next morning. It's so dreary, isn't it? So surely there are better things out there, new adventures to have, new people to meet. Do you ever think about that?"

All the time, Ella silently answered. She contemplated that exact question almost every day, wondering if there was more than this unforgiving bunker and monotonous daily routine. She'd never really felt at home here, if she was brutally honest. But she didn't know how to explain that to Katie.

So instead she said, "I'm not sure. I suppose that yes, there must be better things out there, but it's much easier to just stay here and accept what we have than to stand up and challenge the status quo."

Katie looked thoughtful at this. "Yes, you're right. You have to have courage to take a risk. But what do you suppose the better things out there are? Is there a place you'd like to be?"

This was a difficult question to answer, as there weren't supposed to be any other places to go anymore. It was either here, or the surface, and the surface wasn't exactly the safest place to be. Hadn't the Underground been built as an escape from the horrors of the surface? Hadn't it been designed to be idyllic in every way, utterly perfect, so that you never wanted to leave?

And if truth be told, Ella didn't want really want to leave. This bunker, this unwelcoming, lonely bunker, was the only home she'd ever known, and although deep down she hated being here, she couldn't bring herself to leave. Who knew what awaited in the untamed world above? Anyway, leaving for the surface was heavily discouraged by management. They preferred everyone to be here; Ella often thought that this was more of a prison than a safe haven.

And yet, she couldn't deny that some small part of her was drawn to the surface. She had read about it so much, been told a great deal by her mother- she sort of longed to see it for herself. Sure, it was wild, ruthless and barren, but it also seemed like a kind of freedom. Wide, open expanses, nothing ever the same, no rules to follow. It was everything the Underground wasn't.

But she couldn't say all that to Katie, so she merely replied, "No, there's no place I'd rather be."

However, that question nagged her for the rest of the day, even after she left the unassuming, silent library after work and headed towards the communal area. She took the back door there- there was a shortcut between the two areas at the back of the library, where the private reading rooms were, but not many people knew about it. It was quite nice to have something secret in a setting like the Underground.

The back door took Ella to the corridor that led to the cinema room. This was another reason why most people were unaware of the shortcut- the cinema room was hardly ever used, except by the older residents who missed the surface and spent their days watching old movies. No youth here gave a second thought to the world they might have lived in, if things had gone differently. Ella was almost unique in her study of it.

She walked past the cinema room, past the study area full of students using the computers on the desks, towards the lounge. This was the largest area of the communal space, full of bright red sofas and armchairs, and simple wooden coffee tables. There was a coffee machine by the wall, near the entrance to the meeting rooms. On the concrete floor was a big, round, fluffy gold rug. This décor was the reason she spent most of her time here. It was warm, cosy, inviting. It was pretty much the only room in the entire Underground that was meant to look that way.

The lounge was quite quiet today. There were only three or four other people there. As Ella passed by, one woman, a forgettable thirty-something with brown hair, smiled at her and said, "Good afternoon."

Ella didn't reply, simply nodding in response, and walked towards the furthest armchair away from her. She collapsed into the seat, took her bag off her shoulder and removed her sketchbook from within.

Ella always carried a small sketchbook with her. She was an avid artist, and she especially loved drawing people and things. Her mother always said she could be professional, but Ella had never really been interested in pursuing a career in art. She preferred to just draw in her free time.

Today, though, she was lacking inspiration. She felt heavy and numb, indifferent to what was going on around her. After a moment's thought, she just began to move the pencil with no direction. She didn't think about what she was doing- she just drew. It was a few hours before what she was drawing became clear.

She was drawing herself. It was clearly Ella, but not an Ella she recognised. In the picture, she was beaming, happy and relaxed. She stood in a familiar spot, one she had seen many times in books but never in real life.

She was standing in Paris, the Eiffel Tower clearly visible behind her. She was standing next to a young woman and a man, neither of whom she knew. They, too, were smiling naturally, and the woman had her arm around Ella's shoulder as if they were good friends.

It was such an unusual image; Ella wondered where it had come from. She had drawn it almost instinctively, as if it came from her very soul. It took a little while for something to dawn on her, as she stared at the drawing curiously. This was what she truly wanted from life.

Katie's question from earlier popped back into her mind, without warning, and suddenly she knew how to answer it. This drawing represented her true goal in life. She wanted to live on the surface, in Paris, surrounded by good friends who understood her. She briefly wondered why, in that case, she hadn't drawn Nathan, but she pushed the thought away. She was too preoccupied with this new revelation, and didn't know how to react.

Suddenly, the door in her dream made so much more sense. She realised that the outside seemed like an escape to her, a thrilling adventure. Maybe there was more to that dream than she'd initially thought.

Maybe.

Four

lla slept much better that night. She didn't dream at all, and at eight o'clock, when the wake-up alarm sounded, she felt invigorated and revitalised.

She even looked better this morning, too. Standing in front of the mirror in the bathroom, she noted a glow in her complexion, a natural smile as she gazed at herself.

She had just turned twenty-one, but looked quite young for her age. People often mistook her for eighteen, maybe nineteen. She had a robust nose and full lips, brown eyes shining out of her tanned complexion. She had often been told that she looked very much like her mother, and she was glad of that. She didn't want anything to do with her father, and that included any of his facial features.

As she left the bathroom, the speaker clicked and a male voice started the morning announcements. Ella could've sworn she recognised it, but couldn't place it.

"Good morning, everyone," he said. He was trying to sound jovial, but his voice was too drab and monotonous for that. "It's Saturday the 18th of June, and I have some news to share."

Ella was hardly listening as he told everyone the breakfast special was banana bread and that the kid's craft day would soon be taking place. She didn't have work today, so she put on a light blue dress with white leggings underneath and white casual trainers. She left the room, bag on her shoulder, and walked down the corridor as she did every morning, in the direction of the cafeteria. The man finished the announcements, but the speaker didn't click as usual. He'd obviously forgotten to turn it off. No matter. She carried on walking, but had only taken a few steps when something unusual happened.

Someone else spoke over the speaker, without meaning to, in hushed tones. They were audible- they clearly thought it wasn't still on.

"Are you sure?" That was Megan Masters, but she didn't sound her usual cheery self. Her light, airy voice was full of worry. "I mean, this could be serious… we have to be certain."

Another voice, a man's she didn't recognise. "Yes, we're sure. We double and triple checked. There can't be any doubt. This is bad."

"What do we do?" whispered someone else, panicked. "What do we tell the public? They'll be terrified- they'll want answers."

Ella noticed that everyone else in the corridor had stopped dead in their tracks, staring up at the speaker on the wall. They looked confused and more than a little scared, as if they were under attack but what from, nobody knew. The atmosphere felt heavy and tense, and she realised that she could hardly breathe.

"We have to be careful what we say," Megan was telling the others. Then, unexpectedly, the sound cut out. Someone had turned the speaker off. But even with the conversation now muted, the mood in the corridor was decidedly nervous. Unsure what to do, some people began moving off, slowly, as if afraid something would happen if they moved from that spot.

Nothing did happen, however, and promptly the crowd began to disperse, muttering to each other as they did. Ella supposed she should do the same, so followed everyone else out of Sector Four.

She quickly arrived at the cafeteria, and saw Nathan sat nearby. He was in his work uniform, a blue short-sleeved shirt and black trousers. He was seemingly deep in thought as she approached, having got cereal for herself from the self-service counter.

"Oh, hi, Ella," he said, as she sat down next to him. "I didn't see you there."

"That's fine. I saw you were contemplating something, so I just let you be."

They ate in silence for a little bit. Nathan carried on thinking, looking very concerned, and finally Ella could take no more. "What's bothering you, Nathan? Is something wrong?"

He nodded. "Yes, I think something is wrong. I can't stop thinking about what Megan and the others said over the speaker earlier, and I just think there's a big problem they're not telling us about."

Ella had tried to push away the nagging anxiety caused by the incident earlier. She didn't really want to open that Pandora's box, because she had so many worries on her mind just lately.

However, she nodded in agreement. "I'm worried, too. I just have a feeling that things are going wrong recently. The night before last I had a nightmare about the floor collapsing, and Mum told me I had to leave, I was in danger. I think there's something more to it than I first thought."

She decided not to tell him about the door or her sudden realisation that she wanted to live in Paris. That wasn't pertinent to the conversation, and anyway, she didn't want anyone to know.

"That's interesting," Nathan observed. "I wonder what that means. You've always had good instincts-maybe you sensed something was up before the rest of us."

Ella didn't buy this. True, she had always had good instincts, but she'd never had a dream like that before. Her theory was that her mother had actually come into her dream to warn her about something. Ella did believe in such things as the afterlife.

But now she wanted to change the subject. "Yeah, maybe. Anyway, what are you doing today?"

This was a stupid question, because she knew he was going to work. But she asked it anyway, in the hope of distracting him and cheering him up. He seemed to realise this, but obliged nonetheless. "I'm working today. The computers need debugging and they've asked me to do it. By all accounts, I'm the most qualified."

Nathan worked in the infrastructure department, with the IT. He fixed problems with the sensors and things on the pumps that controlled the air flow throughout the Underground. His was a vital job, because without him there wouldn't be any clean air to breathe and this place would've failed years ago.

He was always very humble about it all, though. *I'm not doing anything special*, he'd say. *I just fix computers all day.*

"That's good," Ella said. "At least you have something to distract you."

"What about you?" he asked. "What are you doing?"

Ella actually wasn't sure. She hadn't decided yet. "I don't know. I suppose I'll go to the library and read, as the communal area is denied me today."

"Ah yes. The children's craft day is today. That's as good a plan as any, I'd say."

Yes, the library, she thought. She could spend some time reading up on Paris. That sounded good. Plus, she could talk to Katie and Jessica. They were on the rota for today.

Nathan checked his watch, taking a last sip of his coffee. "It's almost eight thirty. I better get into work. See you later, Ella."

"Yeah. Bye, Nathan." She smiled a goodbye as he stood up, tucking his chair under the table. He had only taken one step, however, when an alarm started to sound.

It wasn't an alarm she knew. It was not the wake-up and it definitely didn't sound like the fire alarm. It was loud and shrill, and for some strange reason, hearing it struck cold terror into her heart.

Five

The alarm blared for several seconds, then stopped just as suddenly as it had started. An unearthly silence swept the room, each and every person waiting with baited breathe for something to happen next.

They didn't have to wait long. Presently, the speaker clicked, and a tired, anxious voice spoke. Ella was shocked to realise it was Megan's. She sounded as if the weight of the world was on her shoulders; not at all her usual happy self.

"Good morning, everybody," she began. Every word dripped with sadness. "I'm sorry for what happened earlier. We forgot the sound was on- we didn't mean for you to hear. I truly regret any distress it may have caused you."

She chose what she said carefully, Ella noticed. She spoke deliberately and slowly. She'd obviously rehearsed this in advance.

Megan sighed, achingly, and continued. "The reason for the alarm is simple. We didn't mean to frighten you; we just had to get your attention. This is very important and you all need to hear it." She paused, briefly, as if steeling herself, and then said hastily, "The truth is, we believe Thickair has gotten into the Underground."

Nobody reacted for a moment. They simply stared blankly, as if unable to take this in. What did she mean, Thickair had gotten in? That was meant to be impossible. And why now, after twenty-one years? This was utterly incomprehensible.

Megan allowed a few seconds for this to sink in before speaking again. "Earlier this morning, a man from Sector Three was taken into hospital with symptoms similar to that of Thickair poisoning. Doctors have since been able to rule out any other cause for his illness. They're currently treating him in a specialist isolation ward, as a precaution. It is unclear at this time where he might have contracted Thickair poisoning, or if this is an isolated case. For the time being, we think it might be."

Suddenly, hushed whispers broke out across the room. Panic was evident in everyone's faces as they looked around at each other in horror. They seemed to be withdrawing from people at the next table, even, as if the strangers had Thickair and would contaminate them. You could almost taste the terror in the air.

"We know this is scary." Megan sounded louder now, more assertive. "I'm afraid, too. But while we're investigating this, I have to ask you all to remain calm. I know it's hard, but please, try to carry on as normal. I plead with you to trust in me as your Leader to sort this out. I only have your best interests in mind. For now, then, the management team and I would strongly advise the wearing of masks in public spaces. They will be available from the desk in the communal area if you need one. This does unfortunately mean that the craft day will be moved to next Saturday, so that everyone can obtain a mask today should they wish. I will inform you immediately when we have another update, just listen for the alarm. And again, please don't panic. I will get to the bottom of this."

The speaker clicked and she was gone. Ella felt completely numb. She'd listened gravely to every word, but oddly enough, she wasn't scared. She just felt empty, as if she'd been expecting this and she'd just been proven right, but she hadn't wanted to be.

Nathan, however, seemed to be confused. He stood there silently, face as white as a sheet, eyes wide with terror. He was muttering quietly to himself, "No, surely not. That's not possible, is it?"

Ella was concerned by this. "Hey," she said. "You OK?"

It took a moment for him to respond, snapping out of his daze. "Yeah… yeah, I'm fine. I'm just wondering, that's all."

"Wondering about what?" Ella enquired, curious. "A problem shared is a problem halved, after all. If indeed there is a problem."

Nathan shook his head. "I'm not sure there is. I just wonder how it got in. The systems are meant to be foolproof, they were fine when I left them a few days ago. Maybe there's another explanation…"

Ella thought she understood what he was getting at. "You think they might have been tampered with?"

"Possibly. I can't say for certain. More than likely one of the sensors has broken somewhere along the pipeline and let trace amounts of Thickair in. The infrastructure is quite old, I wouldn't be entirely surprised if that were the case."

Ella didn't know what to think. Yes, the logical explanation was that a sensor *had* broken. Nathan had explained to her how the pumps worked one time. They took air from the surface and filtered it clean until there was no Thickair in it at all. It was then distributed into each room every day via a giant tank full of clean air with pipes leading off it. If a sensor broke, this entire system would fail. But he wouldn't have suggested tampering if there wasn't a chance it had happened, slim as that chance was.

The thought made her uncomfortable.

"Well, at least you can investigate that possibility today at work," she stated, trying to keep the worry out of her voice. "That is your job, after all."

"That reminds me," he said, checking his watch. "I'm running late as it is. I'm sorry, Ella- we'll have to talk some other time..."

"That's OK. Go to work." Ella watched him walk away and disappear through one of the eleven metal doors embedded in each of the four walls in the cafeteria. The one Nathan walked to had the words INFRASTRUCTURE painted above it in yellow lettering. He punched a code into the keypad next to it and opened the door, vanishing from her view.

The other people in the room had noticed this and were starting to move off, towards their respective destinations. It was still unusually silent, but everyone seemed to have accepted there was nothing they could do right now and so they just had to go about their day as best they could. Ella remained seated, watching them. Some walked towards RETAIL, others FARMING AND AGRICULTURE. Many went towards COMMUNAL. She noticed a group of students heading towards EDUCATION, despite it being a Saturday. They clearly had some after-school club to go to or something.

Her eyes, however, were drawn to the door labelled HOSPITAL. It was on the opposite side of the room, barely visible. She hadn't been in there for years, except for her six-monthly dentist check-up. She still remembered it well, though.

She recalled the ward her mother was in. She had just turned twelve. Her mother was seriously ill following a heart attack. It had happened so unexpectedly; Ella had been at school when her teacher took her aside to inform her that her mother had collapsed while working as a lifeguard in the leisure centre. She had been rushed to the hospital but was in an unstable condition. Despite her fitness, unbeknownst to even her mother, she had suffered from an underlying heart problem. Ella stayed by her side for a week, but it was no good. She was too weak to carry on.

After her mother's death, Ella was sent to live with her father. She hadn't seen him since she was three, when her parents divorced, and barely remembered him. He wasn't cruel or deliberately hurtful, but he just didn't have time for her. He was distant and cold. She had hated it there in Sector One, especially as her sudden status alienated her from everyone at school. She suddenly had luxuries they didn't and so they stopped talking to her. Only Nathan stood by her, supporting her through her grief and giving her a shoulder to cry on. When she was seventeen, after five years of this, she'd had enough, and left to live on her own in Sector Four. She graduated a year later and became a librarian, and never looked back on those years with her father.

She didn't miss him at all. But right now, in the midst of all this chaos, she wished with all her being that she still had a stable family unit to go to at times like this.

Before

With the apocalyptic weather wreaking havoc on humankind, the last thing anybody needed was Thickair.

The arrival of Thickair marked a new phase of the destruction of humanity. The atmosphere that we had polluted with greenhouse gases now began to evolve something deadly. An invisible poison, ever-present and horrifying.

When the first cases were reported, nobody knew what was going on. These people had been healthy the day before, and now they were bed-ridden, being attacked by something nobody could see. They were pale, coughing and could hardly breathe. As the days wore on, panic set in. They began to fear the worst, and started to hallucinate. Their throats burned but no amount of water would soothe it, and their heart would palpitate without warning. Those around them were bewildered, and doctors could find nothing wrong. The only link they had was that they had gone out the day before, in an oddly thick grey mist.

As more cases were discovered, it was determined that a new illness had been created from the polluted air. It had mutated into a sort of bio-toxin, and once inhaled, even in small amounts, would live in the body, attacking the patient's cells and making them deathly ill. Healthy fit young people were dying from this and the population was scared. They dubbed the new illness 'Thickair', and lived in fear they'd be poisoned by it next.

There had been around four billion people left after the flooding and tropical storms flattened the Earth. Now, Thickair decimated what was left of humankind, and after ten years, only seven hundred and eighty-five million people had survived. The situation was desperate and we needed a solution now. None of the medicines or treatments medics had been trying were working and it became glaringly obvious that we weren't going to be able to find a cure for Thickair. If we were to survive as a species, we'd have to think outside the box. We'd have to get creative.

And so, all the remaining nation's governments came together in a massive summit meeting to discuss what to do next. They'd all been working separately up until now, but they knew it was time to cooperate and find the answer together. Two weeks later, after intensive debate and innumerable suggestions, they decided on one idea. With all the plans put in place, the builders started work...

Six

A *week passed.* Then two. Before Ella knew it, a whole month had gone by. A whole miserable month.

The Underground had descended into disarray. One hundred and fifty-two cases had now been reported, all seemingly random and unconnected. All five Sectors had been affected; if one case appeared in Sector Two on Wednesday, three would be announced in Sector One on the Thursday. Ella had neighbours from Sector Four who had just disappeared one morning, only to hear their names in the morning announcements, among the sick. None had any connection to the others, and nobody had a clue how they had got it. Every time they checked the air quality in any given room, it came up clean. Not a molecule of Thickair to be found.

Equally as strange was the fact that there was no fault with the pumps or sensors. They'd double checked everything and gone through the records of all the air that was pumped through, but there were no discrepancies. To all intents and purposes, they'd never stopped working. There was no reason this should be happening.

But it was, and Ella wanted to understand why.

She had looked at every book in the library dealing with the subject of Thickair. There weren't too many, but there were enough, and maddeningly, they held no answers. Not enough was known about it to speak about it with any kind of certainty. Even with twenty-one years of research having been conducted down here, no scientist could explain it properly.

There had been a theory that it might have escaped from the labs where they researched it. It had given a lot of people hope for a short while that they might have found the cause of all this. But this hope, too, was dashed, when it was revealed that the labs no longer kept samples of Thickair because it had been deemed a security risk. They instead studied its structure from images.

So, all in all, life was very depressing at the moment in the Underground.

With the investigation going nowhere, Megan and the management team put some rules in place. They had said it was for public safety, but a lot of people weren't happy about it.

"You must wear a mask in public places," Megan commanded, her voice weary but authoritative. "It is advisable to own more than one, so that you may wash the other. Screens will placed between the tables in the cafeteria and the sofas in the communal area, to prevent mixing. Lights out will be earlier, at seven thirty pm instead of eight, and you will be expected to be in your rooms by that time. If found to be a persistent rule-breaker, you may face punishment. This could include a fine, a docking of your salary or a few days in Sector Five at the most. I hate to do this to you, but it's for your own security. I hope therefore that you will do your utmost to abide by these rules. I also wish to assure you that I will be following them as well, and I too face consequences should I not obey them."

But Megan was losing favour fast with the citizens of the Underground. They saw these measures as overly draconian and were not impressed by her acting in a controlling way. She was using her power more and more, and people didn't like it. She was becoming less diplomatic.

Ella personally thought that Megan was choosing her words too carefully. She used to be so carefree and acted like she wasn't the Leader at all, but just somebody who was your slightly more powerful friend. Now all her speech was pre-prepared, she was clearly trying to be dominant and was becoming more distant as she did so.

But Ella didn't want to dwell on such things. She spent most of her time in her room now, drawing or reading. Sometimes she spent a day with Nathan, but as he got more and more busy with work, he didn't have as much time to spend with her. She understood and accepted this, but it hurt a little. Even with his constant assurances that he did want to talk to her, he just couldn't, she still felt left out. Everyone in her life had left her or ignored her, and she craved human contact more than anything these days. She had got used to being lonely, but that didn't mean she liked being alone.

Even Katie couldn't talk as much anymore. Sam had caught Thickair and a distraught Katie was either at work in the library or by his side in the hospital. Jessica was spending more time with her fiancée and therefore wasn't at the library that much. Ella had nobody to talk to and she hated it.

So she chose to sit in her room most days and draw. If she was going to be alone, she might as well be alone and doing something she loved. Her drawings became more and more abstract as time went on- what started out as recognisable things, like a woman in the library or her room, changed into more unusual pieces. She drew a city one day, a silhouetted urban landscape with grand mountains forming the backdrop. The sun was setting over the tallest mountain, and there was a distant forest leading to a river. She realised this was the city her mother had talked about on the surface, the one that was just a half hour away on foot from the bunker's exit. She vaguely remembered seeing a picture of it in a book one time and this matched it exactly. She must have subconsciously retained that image.

However, on the morning of Monday the 18th of July she didn't feel like drawing. She had had work the previous day and it had been awful. Katie had been visibly upset and told Ella that Sam was not doing well, that he was now on an oxygen mask to breathe. She was therefore not in a great mood and just wanted to lie on her bed with her eyes closed.

So that's exactly what she did, not moving a muscle until well past midday. She got up to get lunch in the cafeteria, slipping on a grey face mask as she left the room. It was pretty much deserted, so she chose a seat next to the wall. She had got herself a chocolate cake and a ham sandwich to eat, and after she had finished her somewhat underwhelming meal she returned to her room and lay back on her bed, totally silent.

It wasn't until two o'clock that something disturbed her peace. There was a knock on her door, a sharp *rap, rap*. She sat up quickly, staring around at the room as if the person was inside with her.

Another knock, slightly louder this time.

This was quickly followed by muffled footsteps walking away hurriedly. Ella rushed to the door to see who was there, but she was too late. By the time she opened the door, the corridor outside was empty. Not a soul to be seen. Probably just some kid playing tricks on her. She was about to turn to go back inside when she noticed a small envelope on the floor by her feet.

Intrigued, she bent down to pick it up. Closing the door and sitting back down on her bed, she noticed there was writing on the envelope. Her name, in neat handwriting.

ELLA.

This was most interesting. She didn't recognise the writing. Inside, there was a letter, written on a generic piece of lined paper.

Don't believe what you've been told. Come to room 517, Sector Four, at eight thirty pm tonight. Door combination is 935189. Don't be afraid. Don't tell anyone.

We're going to stop Thickair.

That was it.

"What the-?" she murmured to herself, under her breath. She couldn't believe what she was reading. This was insane. This was like a conspiracy. People like her didn't get secretive letters inviting her to a clandestine night-time meeting. What did they want with *her*, of all people? Was this a trap?

There was only one way to find out. Trap or not, she'd just have to go and see for herself.

Seven

The rest of the day seemed to drag by. Ella's nerves were in knots, nervously waiting for eight thirty to come. At seven pm, there a rush of footsteps outside her door. Lots of people were coming and going before the lights went off. At half past, there was no sound from outside at all, and promptly the lights were switched off.

For the next hour, she sat on her bed with her back against the cold stone wall, thinking about whether she really should go to meet this person. After all, she didn't know who they were. What if it was a trap, as she had first thought? She couldn't help thinking this was incredibly stupid.

On the other hand, something told her that this meeting would change her life forever. She knew in her heart she had to go, despite her misgivings. She just knew this was destiny at work.

So, at eight twenty five, she set off, creeping out her room quietly as a mouse.

She had the note clasped in her right hand. She didn't know where room 517 was precisely, but it wasn't far from hers. She lived in room 503, and 504 was just to the left of hers, leading down the corridor. She didn't usually go down that far because the cafeteria was the other way, but soon she had located 517.

It looked just like all the other doors around it. Unassuming grey metal. The only difference was that the rooms next to it were completely dark and silent, but 517 was not. There was a sliver of light coming out from under the door, and if she put her ear to it, she could vaguely hear someone talking to themselves.

She located the keypad beside the door, but didn't immediately input the code. She felt wary of what waited inside. This could be risky. But at the same time, it could answer all her questions. It felt like a life-defining moment.

She put in the code. 935189.

It worked. The door clicked and opened slightly, allowing her entry. She took a deep breath and pushed it open.

Inside was a room exactly like hers. Same bed in the corner, same wardrobe and desk, same analogue clock on the wall. That was what she had been expecting. What she had not been expecting was the woman sat at the circular table.

This was clearly her room, but still Ella was surprised to see her. She looked up as Ella entered, cautiously, and smiled warmly. "Hello, Ella," she said in greeting. "It's wonderful to finally meet you."

She didn't look very threatening. She was probably about five years older than Ella, but no more than that. She had curly blonde hair and dazzling tourmaline blue eyes. She smiled naturally and radiated joy and friendliness. But appearances could be deceptive, and so Ella remained suspicious.

"Likewise," Ella replied, slowly. "If I may ask, who are you? Why am I here?"

"I'm Amy," the woman responded kindly. "As for why you're here, that'll be explained in a minute. The secrecy is regrettable, but necessary, I assure you. He'll be here soon to explain everything. Please remain calm."

She sounded like Megan. That irritated Ella, and she felt a surge of anger. Who was she to tell her to be calm? This was highly unorthodox and she had a right to be as frightened as she pleased! She opened her mouth to speak, but was cut off by the sound of the door opening.

Ella turned around to face the newcomer, her fury replaced by an icy fear. Was this the 'he' Amy had mentioned? Who was 'he'?

This question was answered when a man walked into the room. He glanced at Ella and nodded a hello, then turned to Amy and addressed her. "Hello again. I see you delivered the note."

This informal, casual tone contrasted entirely with Ella's reaction to his appearance. She stared, shocked, at him. Of all the people in the entirety of the Underground, this was the last person she'd ever expect to see here.

It was Nathan.

Her best friend Nathan, who was now conversing with Amy as if this was all completely normal. "Of course I gave her the note," Amy was saying. "I didn't let her see me, naturally. The security of our mission is of paramount importance."

Nathan nodded in agreement. "Yes, it is. You did a good job getting Ella here. Thank you."

This was getting too weird. Finally regaining the power of speech, all she could think of to say, out of the hundreds of questions she had in mind, was, "I am here, you know. Do you mind not talking about me like I'm a ghost or something?"

Nathan turned to look at her at this. "Yes, sorry, Ella. I know this is confusing, but I promise you there's a good reason for all this."

"There better be!" Ella wasn't angry anymore, more upset at Nathan's choice of meeting. She felt he'd deceived her somehow. "I've been dragged out of my room at night, illegally, to some top secret meeting, only being told something about Thickair and some mission you're on. You'd better explain yourself or I'm leaving."

Nathan and Amy looked at each other, as if using telepathy to decide how best to approach this. "It's hard to explain. No, hear me out," he said, as Ella raised her eyebrows in incredulity. "You won't believe us at first, but trust me, I know what I'm doing. I wouldn't put your friendship on the line over nothing."

Ella couldn't believe what she was hearing, but listened intently regardless. "Alright. I'll listen. What's going on here?"

"We believe we know how Thickair got in." Amy was speaking now. Ella still didn't fully trust her, but did not interrupt. "Nathan didn't say anything before because it would have been too risky to tell you in public. You were close, though, with your guess before that someone had tampered with the pumps."

Ella wanted to ask how she knew that, but didn't. Instead she enquired, "How was I close? How did it get in?"

"There's a traitor among us." This was such an absurd statement, Ella couldn't take it in. What did she mean, a traitor? Who ever heard of such a thing? "Someone has been indoctrinated by a group of rebels on the surface to destroy this place. They put Thickair into the pumps and modified the IT systems so that no-one can trace it, not even Nathan. They have total control over where it goes and who falls ill."

Ella scoffed derisively. "A traitor? Come on. How can you prove that?"

"I wish we could," Nathan said. "But unfortunately, the only CCTV footage of the traitor putting the Thickair into the pumps has been deleted. Amy was the only one person to see it before the traitor realised they were captured on camera. Amy came straight to me with the information, realising I suspected something, and fearing the traitor would find out she saw the footage."

"That's…" Ella didn't know what to say. This was too much for her. "Who has that kind of power? I mean, who can control the IT, direct the Thickair and then delete the evidence?"

But as soon as she asked the question, she realised she knew exactly who. Nathan saw the look of horror on her face, and correctly guessed what she was thinking. "That's right. The traitor is Megan Masters."

Eight

A *moment of silence followed this announcement.*

Ella didn't know how to react. This was unbelievable. Megan Masters, a traitor... how could that be?

"Why?" she managed to say, voice trembling. "Why would Megan do that?"

"Well, the rebel group we mentioned earlier really hate the Underground. They want this place gone. When we all moved here twenty-one years ago, they were left behind to try to fix the world, and they feel abandoned. You know the founding principle of friendship? That originally referred to a trade relationship with the surface. We promised to help them survive on their own in such a harsh world, and in turn they provided goods for us. After about a year, we were producing enough goods of our own to support ourselves, and the management team cut ties with the surface dwellers. They've hated us ever since.

And in recent years, a group emerged. They are radicals, they believe violence solves everything. We think they sent someone down here posing as a citizen and they got to Megan. They brainwashed her and when the Leadership elections came, they made sure she got put into office."

"Yes," Amy sighed sadly. "But the trouble is, nobody would believe us. We'd be sent to Sector Five for good."

That was true. Who in their right mind would take the word of three Sector Four residents over that of the *Leader*?

"So what do we do?" Ella was confused. If they couldn't stop Megan, what was there to do? They were just normal people. They couldn't do anything about this.

Nathan seemed to pick up on her doubts. "We're not helpless to stop this. In fact, we might be the most qualified."

"What do you mean?" Nothing was making sense.

"We need to identify the fake citizen. The group has somebody down here and even if we did take down Megan, they'd just brainwash the next Leader. If we can get their name and face, we can stop all of this."

"OK. How do we do that?" Ella was excited. She had something to do, a dangerous task. She felt like a spy in an action movie.

"We haven't got anywhere with our surveillance down here," Amy said. "The time has come for a new plan. We have to go direct to the source."

"You mean-?"

"Yes. We have contacts on the surface who may have information. To obtain that information, we have to go to them. That means leaving the Underground for a little while."

This floored Ella. Although deep down she longed to leave and seek adventure, she hadn't actually considered that she *could*. She didn't even know how people left; nobody knew where the exit was anymore.

And to go to the surface... while a thrilling notion in many ways, she wasn't sure she had the courage to. When push came to shove, she didn't think she was capable of it.

"I understand," Nathan said gently, noting her dumbfounded expression. "This is a shock. We don't expect anything of you. All we want is to ask you along. We could really use your help on this."

"What help could I be? I mean, I'm not special or anything. What can I possibly offer you?"

Amy smiled at this. "Nathan's told me all about you. That you have good instincts and that you're more knowledgeable about the surface than most people your age." Ella wasn't sure she agreed with this, but allowed Amy to continue. "We'd be incredibly grateful if you'd be willing to share that knowledge with us. We won't force you, though."

Ella considered for a second. "Say if I did agree to go. What would we be doing? What would my role be?"

Nathan answered this question. "Well, the first day we'd go in search of our contacts. We'd try to persuade them to help us. If they agree, we follow their lead. If not, well, we just have to look elsewhere for answers."

"We have some others in our group," Amy elaborated. "Each of us will have different roles. We'll explain more if you decide to come."

Ella nodded. This didn't entirely satisfy her, but she understood why they were so tight-lipped. This was a risky business, after all.

"OK. So, where would I go if I decided to come with you? When are you leaving?"

"A week from now, on Monday the 25th. We'll all gather here in my room at precisely five am for a debrief. We have to leave in the early hours so nobody sees us. We'll bring food and things like that, so all you'll need is clothes and essentials. We don't know how long we'll be out there for."

This didn't exactly fill Ella with confidence. They didn't really have a plan, by the sounds of it. She'd have to consider this carefully before coming to a decision.

She exhaled deeply, thinking. "I'll think about it." She wasn't going to make any promises. "I'm not saying if I'm going or not. I won't tell anyone about this, though. I won't jeopardise the mission in any way."

Nathan and Amy looked relieved at this, both visibly relaxing. "Thank you. Come to a decision in your own time. You have to feel right about leaving. If you don't want to take the risk, you don't have to. But we'd love to have you on the team."

The team. That was an interesting choice of word, Ella thought. It suggested that they needed her, that she was letting the side down if she didn't come. It was almost reverse psychology, telling her it was fine to stay while secretly guilt-tripping her into going. But almost as soon as she thought this, she pushed it away. She was reading too much into this. They were probably just eager to get her support and getting carried away.

Five minutes later, she was back in her room, lying in her bed. She couldn't sleep. Nathan had left first, and Ella swiftly followed, Amy saying a last 'good night' before the door closed. She had crept back here silently, not making a sound as she tiptoed down the gloomy dark corridor, and had collapsed into her bed without bothering to change into her pyjamas. She was suddenly tired and just wanted some rest.

She didn't get it, though. She tossed and turned all night, sleeping in short fitful bursts and always waking up an hour or so later. She just couldn't switch off. Her mind was churning, filled to the brim with thoughts of the surface. Finally, at one am, she gave in and stared at the ceiling, pondering.

This eventually led to thoughts of her mother. What would she have said? Ella wished right now that she could talk to her, get her advice on this. She remembered the dream, and wondered if the ominous message in it might have been referring to this exact situation.

Run, Ella. Leave here now. You are in terrible danger. Get out of here now. Seek...

What did 'seek' mean? Seek what? As she noticed her eyelids feeling heavy and sleep tugging at her brain, she mused that perhaps it meant seeking the surface as she had done in her dream.

And then, suddenly, she was asleep.

Nine

E lla tried so hard over the course of the next few days to convince herself it was all an absurd dream. Just her imagination. After all, such things didn't happen in real life, did they?

But in her heart she knew she was kidding herself. It had really happened, so she had to make a decision. The choice was agonising.

It didn't help that cases of Thickair poisoning had almost quadrupled in just five days. Six hundred and seven people were now in hospital, many barely holding on. Tragically, seventy eight had died, including the man from Sector Three who had been the first to be hospitalised.

To make matters worse, the morning announcements just got more and more depressing as management tried to get a grip on the situation.

"We have been lenient thus far," a man said one day, the same drab-voiced man Ella vaguely thought she knew. "No longer. For your own safety, we are tightening the rules. You must not be out of your room at all after hours unless you are working or have a good reason. You must stay in your room until you have to go to work, or until the wake-up, whichever is earlier. We will be issuing devices to each household that allow you to check the air quality in your room when you enter. If it is found to be at an unsafe level, report it to us immediately and do not enter. We will find you alternative accommodation if we cannot fix the issue. Guards will be enforcing these rules and you will face punishment if caught to be breaking them."

This had not gone down well with the public at all, and there was an outcry to have Megan kicked out of office. Ella did not join in, not wanting to raise suspicion, and merely listened as the people around her booed when her voice came over the speaker. She handled it well, though. Being a traitor probably meant she didn't care what anyone thought of her.

Nathan was remarkably quiet these days, too. As Monday drew near, she saw less and less of him, and when she did, he didn't say a word about the mission.

His demeanour had changed, he smiled less. He seemed to be studying her, trying to gauge what she was going to do.

On Sunday she had still not decided, and she was getting stressed.

She wandered around vaguely, not fully comprehending what she was doing so that half an hour later she would be somewhere and wondered how she got there. Her head was screaming at her to be sensible, to stay here and take her chances. Her heart urged her to go, to follow her dream. They pulled her in different directions, both just as strong as the other, until she didn't know what she wanted anymore.

"Are you OK, miss?"

The voice startled her out of her thoughts. It was a moment before she realised that there was someone talking to her. It was a woman. Ella suddenly recognised her as the one who had said good afternoon to her that day she drew the picture of Paris. She stared, concerned, at Ella, a slight frown curling her mouth.

Ella had ignored her the first time, but today she really needed to talk to someone. "Yeah, I'm fine. Just thinking."

"Haven't we all? It's been such a difficult few weeks; it's madness at the moment." She seemed talkative, eager to have a conversation with just about anybody. Such people usually annoyed Ella, but right now she completely understood and complied.

"Yes, it's been crazy."

The woman suddenly looked contemplative. "You know, you look familiar. I thought so before, but now I definitely think I've seen you somewhere before."

She probably had. This place was big, but the population was in such close quarters it wasn't unusual to see the same people every day. Still, this statement intrigued her slightly.

Then the woman's face lit up as if a light bulb had gone off in her head. "Yes, that's it! You're Samantha Castley's daughter, aren't you? Ellie, or something like that?"

"Ella. And yes, I am." This was most interesting. How did this woman know her mother? How did she know her, more to the point?

This question was answered a second later. "I'm Leanne Foster. I was your mother's best friend. I used to take my daughter Naomi to play dates with you. Do you remember?"

Now that she mentioned it, Ella did have a faint memory of play dates with a girl called Naomi. She had lost contact with both her and her mother when she was sent to live with her father. Leanne had been at her mother's funeral, actually. She had sat in the back row, sobbing quietly- Ella recalled Leanne comforting her as she left. How could she have forgotten her?

Leanne was speaking again now. "I haven't seen you in years. You look so mature and beautiful. Your mother would be proud." Ella smiled at this, a burst of happiness glowing inside her. She was glad she'd met Leanne. "How have you been these days?"

"Oh, fine, really." She was lying, but she didn't want to burden her with the truth of what her life was really like. "I left to live on my own at seventeen. I work as a librarian and I couldn't be happier. Anyway, how are you? What's Naomi doing?"

"We're doing OK. I lost Pete, my husband, seven years ago, but we're coping well. Naomi's just turned twenty-three and is a doctor at the hospital. Her brother Jacob is sixteen and works part-time in a shop. He wants to be a scientist when he graduates."

"That's good. You must be proud of them, doing such worthwhile things." She paused, and then added, sadly, "I'm just a librarian. I sometimes wish I could do something special, help people like they are."

"You're not just a librarian," Leanne said. "You're worthwhile, too. You don't have to be a doctor or a scientist to help people. Cheering just one person up or doing one good deed is more than enough."

Ella understood what she was trying to say. You didn't have to be great to do great things. You just had to believe you were a valuable person, and you could do anything.

And she suddenly realised she'd made a decision. She would go with the others on the mission. She could do something great, something truly worthwhile that would benefit a lot of people. Nobody ever did anything good without taking some risks. She would do something risky and put herself in danger, to save other people from that selfsame danger. It was a worthy cause.

She wouldn't pretend she wasn't frightened. But nothing worth doing is easy. In life, you can take the easy path and let life control you or you can take the right path, and be in the driver's seat instead of the passenger's. For a long time, she had taken the easy path and it had led her to loneliness and melancholy.

Now she would take the right path and she was excited to see what awaited her on the surface. This was her destiny and it was about time she seized it.

"Yes," she said. "You're right. I'm not just a librarian. I'm strong and intelligent. And I'm going to do something worthwhile with my life."

Leanne nodded approvingly. "That's all your mother ever would've wanted from you. She wanted you to be happy and follow your heart. She wanted the best for you. Whatever you do, she'll be looking down on you and smiling."

Ella made a mental note to catch up with Leanne and Naomi when she got back. She'd missed them, she realised, and desperately wanted that kind of social interaction in her life. They exchanged details and said goodbye, and Ella headed back towards her room to wait for Monday to come.

Ten

The rest of the day seemed to fly past. Ella sat in her room, on the edge of her bed, her stomach both knotting with nerves and soaring weightlessly with exhilaration. She tried to draw to calm herself down, but it was no good, so she just sat there silently, thinking.

At seven thirty pm, the lights were switched off as usual. At around eight, there came the sound of guards patrolling the corridor outside, no doubt looking for rule breakers. Ella could hear their footsteps on the concrete and see the flash of their torches through the crack in her door. She wondered, briefly, if she'd be able to get out at all, but at around ten pm the footsteps faded away and stopped completely.

She tried to get some sleep but for what seemed to be the umpteenth time, she was unable to switch off. She lay in bed fully clothed, dressed in jeans and a jumper, with a thin coat on over the top. A backpack stood on the central table, filled with clothes and some personal effects she couldn't bear to leave behind. This included her sketchbook and pencils, and a photo of her and her mother that usually stood on the tall shelving unit.

She eventually managed to doze off into a shallow sleep, but was rudely awakened a few hours later by her alarm. Four fifty am. She quickly shut off the alarm to avoid waking anyone else up, and got up quickly, a new energy and resolve filling her. She slung the backpack onto her shoulders, checked she had everything, and left the room.

She knew the way to room 517 by now and found it within two minutes. She inputted the code, enthusiasm building inside her, and bounded through the door into the room.

"Ah, Ella," Amy said as she entered. "I'm so glad you could come."

There was a small group of people inside. She recognised Nathan and Amy immediately, but there were two other people she didn't know. There was a man stood nearby talking to Nathan. He was probably about thirty-five to forty, if Ella had to guess, with unkempt dark brown hair and a surly face. He looked as if he could curdle dairy, and she promptly resolved not to cross him.

Sat in a chair next to Amy was a much kinder looking young woman. She couldn't have been any more than eighteen, and had a friendly face and long silky black hair. She caught Ella's eye and grinned, and Ella smiled back, naturally. She could tell they were going to be good friends.

As Ella walked over to the table and joined the throng, the chatter died down and everyone turned to face her. The surly man spoke first. "You're Ella?"

Taken aback by his curtness, all she could manage to say in reply was, "Yeah, I am. And you are?"

"Matt." He spoke bluntly and in short sentences, as if wary of talking for too long. Ella wasn't entirely sure she liked this Matt character. "It's good to meet you. Nathan's told us all about you."

No. She definitely didn't like him. Even when he was trying to be polite, he sounded gruff and impatient, as if he didn't want you in his way.

"Hi, I'm Lacey," the kind young woman piped up. "I'm glad you're here. I hear you have unsurpassed knowledge of the surface and the way it works."

"I suppose so, yes."

"Oh, don't be so modest, Ella," Nathan interjected on her behalf. "Your mother taught you well. Most people our age don't bother to even try to learn about the surface."

Lacey looked at Ella approvingly, a warm shine in her eyes. "It's good that you and your mother had something to bond over. My parents taught me all about the surface, too, but not about its customs. I have an encyclopaedic knowledge of the geography of the city and its surrounding areas. I'm a walking, talking map, if you will." She laughed nervously, wringing her hands. "I've never been, though. I grew up here. When I heard about this, I knew I had to go for it and face my fears."

Ella was impressed. Lacey was not even nineteen and she was daring to go with the group because she wanted to expand her horizons. Ella was twenty-one and had only decided to go about twelve hours ago!

"I, on the other hand, have been there before." Matt was talking now, in his usual brusque tone. "I lived on a farm with my parents. It's tough up there. I fell in with the wrong crowd at sixteen. I decided at eighteen that enough was enough. I cut ties with my parents and the group I was a part of, and I moved here for a better life. That's why I'm on this mission.

I have inside knowledge of the group responsible for all this."

"We all have clear roles here," Nathan added. "I'm surveillance and intelligence. I've been studying this group for a while now and I know almost everything about them. You are our guide to what goes on up there. And Amy has some old friends in the city who we're hoping might help us."

Noting Ella's confusion, Amy quickly clarified. "I used to live up there, too. I moved here with my parents when I was fifteen, ten years ago." She looked suddenly sad at the memory. "My best friend Catherine was distraught. She might not help us, but I have to try. I miss her greatly."

This was the first piece of information she had learnt about the mysterious Amy, and it intrigued Ella. But Nathan was suddenly gathering some papers that were scattered around the table and was now explaining what would happen next. She snapped her attention back to him.

"Right then." There were innumerable papers everywhere, some with maps drawn on them, or lists of names or places. Many were just random pages of notes written in the same distinctive handwriting as on that note Ella had received. She supposed it was

Amy's. "We're leaving in about ten minutes. We'll head out of Sector Four and along this corridor" (Ella followed his finger along the map dutifully) "and we'll arrive at this point here. You might have noticed this door before. It *says* it's a maintenance cupboard, but in reality it's the entrance to the exit passageway. That passage leads to the check-in room, and beyond that is a decontamination chamber. That was to cleanse off any Thickair molecules from the people arriving. Then we get to that lift, and it takes us up to the surface. Any questions, anyone?"

There were millions of questions swirling around in Ella's head, but she asked the most troubling one. "Why did they pretend it was a maintenance cupboard? What's the point in that?"

Nathan sighed heavily. "They want to disguise it. Once you're here, they don't want you to leave, and so they hide the exit so that you don't know how to leave. It's a way of controlling you and keeping you here."

She suddenly wished she hadn't asked. This was not the answer she had been expecting. She had always felt trapped here, true, but she'd never felt *controlled* in any way. If she had truly wanted to leave before now, she would have just asked. That was supposed to be everyone's right, to be able to return to the surface if they so wished. When had management lost its way so badly? When did this place become the prison she had always feared it was?

Her exultation was suddenly replaced by nausea, her heart heavy and mournful. In that moment, she was itching to get out, to escape the shackles that had held her back all these years.

She was ready to explore.

Eleven

After the group had made their final preparations, they were ready to leave.

Nathan went out first, to check the coast was clear. Ella waited with the others, anxious to get out, and didn't hesitate for a second when Nathan came back and told them it was safe to proceed.

The five of them walked for several minutes, winding and twisting their way out of Sector Four. They arrived at the main corridor and instead of turning right, towards the cafeteria, they went left, towards Sectors One, Two and Three. Nathan had pointed this way on the map, and so she knew they were headed towards the end of the corridor, where Sector One stood to the right and EDUCATION to the left.

Each Sector was a self-contained square made up of smaller individual rooms. They occupied the entire south space of the Underground, if you took the cafeteria as the central point. Five was the smallest, and served as the prison. It could house up to ten thousand people, or so she heard. Four, where she lived, was slightly smaller than Three and Two, but only just. Four was for singles old enough to live on their own, and often acted as temporary housing until you moved to Three. Three was for couples, and this too sometimes acted as a gateway into Sector Two. You only lived there if you had children, or on the odd occasion, they'd move older people out of Three or Four into Two if they had custody of their grandchildren. Finally, Sector One housed the elite- the rich, the powerful, management and the current Leader. She had lived there with her father for five years, and had led a life of relative luxury, but it had isolated her from all her school friends who were envious of everything she had. She would have traded that private library and cafeteria for just a few friends in a heartbeat.

But now they walked past each of these, and stopped at a dead end. Or so it seemed. Because right there, just as Nathan had said, was a door. It was made of the usual grey metal, with a keypad beside it, but the difference was it had letters written on it in yellow. They said 'CLEANING FACILITIES- DO NOT ENTER'.

The letters were old and peeling. They had clearly been there a long time, unloved and forgotten. But there was something unusual about it. The keypad, she realised upon closer inspection, was fake. Instead, the door had a small keyhole, built in so well that if you weren't looking for it you'd miss it. She recognised that it was a keyhole because she had seen pictures of them in books, but she'd never seen one in real life before. They didn't exist anymore. They were an antiquated notion, a relic of a bygone age. Keypads were more secure and reliable. Where did one even find a key anymore?

Somewhere, obviously, because Amy had it. She took one out of her pocket and fit it into the lock. She stared, fascinated, at the key, as it somehow made the door unlock and swing open. Amy removed it from the lock and put it back in her pocket, and motioned for the group to follow her.

They did so, and emerged into a massive corridor. It was wider than the one they'd just left, and here the lights were still on, though they were flickering somewhat. No-one had been here in years, by the looks of it. It was actually kind of creepy, like a scene in a horror movie when the hero wanders through the abandoned house. Cobwebs could be seen near the ceiling and their footsteps echoed off the walls. She was relieved when they reached another door and came into the check-in room, but this did nothing to help the spooky atmosphere.

The check-in room was enormous. It was probably half the size of the cafeteria, but still it stretched for ages, and it was filled to the brim with desks, chairs and filing cabinets. There were cobwebs and dust on every surface, and the lights were barely giving off any illumination at all. This was clearly where they'd signed in each person, but it hadn't been used in years. The computers on the desks had long been turned off, and there were empty coffee cups still there, waiting to be put in the bin by their owners.

If this was the kind of room required to process the *survivors* of humanity, what kind of population was there now, after twenty-one years? How many were on the surface?

They'd find out soon enough. The group crossed the room quickly to find not a metal door like the one they'd just come through, but a kind of giant circular door not unlike the ones you might find on a submarine. It was apparently opened and closed by a big wheel. It looked stiff and rusty. Ella wasn't sure it could even move anymore.

Matt stepped forward to try. He grabbed the wheel with both hands and pushed it, with all his effort. To her surprise, it groaned slightly before turning in a circle without complaint. When it had gone a full 360 degrees, the door opened obligingly and they were allowed through. They walked straight through the decontamination chamber and into a lift. Ella's wonder at such a marvellous contraption was short-lived when it became clear that it was old and shaky. It swung violently on its way up, moaning and creaking, and she felt quite sick by the time it came to a stop five minutes later.

Fighting off her motion sickness and swirling vision, she stumbled out and didn't notice for several minutes where she was. When she did, she stood in complete amazement, gazing in awe.

This must be the surface. Behind her was the lift, encased in a big metal box, but in front of her was the world her mother had so often talked about.

It wasn't yet dawn here, so the sky was dotted with a few scattered stars. They looked like diamonds, embossed on a velvet cloth that went forever, as far as the eye could see. They stood in a field; there was sweet-smelling grass under her shoes, and a cool breeze on her face. She relished the sensation, it was so different to what she was used to. And there in front of her was the city's silhouette, tall and dominant in the landscape. There was the familiar mountain range behind it, a majestic backdrop that perfectly accompanied the buildings in the forefront. A path led away from the field, a gate in the emerald hedgerow backing onto a dirt path that led directly to the city. Just past her line of sight was the forest, just as vast and beautiful as her mother had said, and beyond came the sound of babbling water. The river.

This was all so much, so stunning and new, but there was something wrong. The gentle wind blowing her hair to and fro smelt a little. She couldn't discern what, but it had a funny odour to it. Was that normal? And now she thought on it, the river too had a toxic stench; perhaps all the sewage and pesticides her mother said used to get dumped in it. Not only that, but the air felt a bit humid, a bit sticky. She gagged a little, not used to such variation in air temperature.

This, then, was a place of beauty and danger. It was deceptively gorgeous. You were drawn to its attractive exterior, but forgot about its deadly interior. There was a reason everyone left in the first place. This was not a place to be messed with.

Nathan suddenly spoke, making her jump. "It's good weather today. That's lucky. We were hoping to avoid a Thickair fog or acid rain."

Thickair fog? Acid rain? She suddenly had serious misgivings about this, but she'd come too far to back out now. She'd had a taste of the surface, its dual personality, and she wanted to know more.

"Yes," Amy replied. "But we have to get moving. The weather changes fast out here. Masks on, just in case."

They did as she said, pulling their face masks over their mouths and noses, and started to head off towards the city. She felt nervous anticipation as she walked down the dirt path, marvelling at everything as she went. This was such a big unknown; she didn't know what would happen next. All she did know was that she was ready for this challenge. *Bring it on*, she thought.

And as she walked, she thought she felt her mother beside her, encouraging her to carry on.

Before

he governments had come up with a plan. They would unite the remaining population of the world into one massive city which would serve as a hub for the builders. Once the city had been completed, they would start work on a massive underground complex to shelter those who had survived.

This plan was controversial and costly, and naturally there was some opposition. But it was swiftly quashed and the plans went ahead on schedule. A city was chosen at random to be the base point for the builders to expand on, and a global alliance was formed. It took over thirty years to complete the city, and time had not been kind to humanity. What had started out as seven hundred and eighty five million people had become less than ninety million. There was an outcry to halt the plans and find a better way but these voices were ignored and the first hole was dug in the construction of the Underground.

It took yet another forty years to perfect this, and the human race was barely holding on. Thickair had taken no prisoners and there were countless casualties. Just three hundred thousand people now remained. Public desperation for safety was at fever pitch and once the last pipe was in place, there was a mad rush to get inside. People left everything behind in order to be saved from certain extinction.

Of course, not everyone went. There were a stubborn few who preferred to stay where they were and tough it out, and they were not forced to leave. Instead, the new Leader of the new management team decreed that henceforth, the Underground and the surface would be allies, relying on each other for trade. The four founding principles of trust, friendship, democracy and hard work would shine though and make the world a better place.

Within a year, this alliance crumbled and snapped completely. The surface renounced the Underground as evil and despicable, and refused to have anything more to do with them. They would look after themselves, as the new citizens of the bunker had learnt to do. In turn, the citizens were encouraged to warn their children never to go to the surface. They didn't want anyone helping the rebels; they needed those children to become good compliant citizens like their parents. Indeed, most did. Scared off by their parent's stories, they found jobs and homes in the Underground, and life was peaceful.

Except one young boy grew curious about the outside world and decided, one night, to sneak out and see it for himself...

Twelve

It didn't take long to reach the city. Half an hour later, the dirt had turned into tarmac, and the hedgerows into buildings. They followed a road into the main thoroughfares, under Lacey's direction, and went into some winding side streets. It was like a gigantic maze.

Everything was so strange here, too. Of course Ella knew what everything was, having studied the surface fervently, but she still found it odd. This was nothing like the bunker. Cars were parked on the side of the road, left by the driver seemingly in a hurry. Some still had keys inside. If Ella could drive, she could easily have taken one. Streetlights lined the pavements, and traffic lights, long since deactivated, showed a singular red circle. Shop fronts were smashed and glass littered the street; money lay on the ground. This was the strangest thing of all to

Ella. The Underground used coupons as currency-your salary was paid straight into an account and you took it out in token form. Here, notes littered the ground, green and with somebody's face on it. Numbers in the corner indicated their value. This was all so bizarre.

Lacey took them through dark damp-smelling alleyways, and wide roads with yellow lines pained faintly in the middle. They walked past skyscrapers and little houses on corners, their windows with curtains pulled over as if someone still lived there. She didn't like this place. It was, in many ways, the closest thing to the Underground up here, and that was why it disturbed her so much. She suddenly longed for the tranquillity of the forest.

Presently Lacey stopped, at the end of an alley. It was tight and claustrophobic, with high dark brick walls on either side. In front of them was a door, a thick one made of rusting metal, and a sliding hatch at the top. Lacey stepped forward and knocked on it three times, sharply. A minute later, the hatch opened and a pair of eyes could be seen through them.

They surveyed the group, frowningly, and then asked, "Who are you and what do you want?"

Lacey answered this question, her voice loud and clear through the mask. "We have travelled from the Underground. We seek an audience with Joe and Catherine."

A grunt from the other side of the door. "Very well. Enter." It swung open to reveal a man standing there, looking rather worse for wear. His dark hair had specks of grey in it, and his face was worn and worried-looking. His eyes sagged and his clothes were ragged and dirty. He gestured for them to follow him.

They descended down a set of stairs. The steps were small and there were no handrails, so Ella ran her hand along the wall to keep her balance. After going down two flights, they reached a basement level. They were met with a large dark room. It seemed to be some sort of lounge, as it had sofas and a table in it, but the rest of the room was full of boxes and packages of some description. A single bulb light shone weakly overhead. Their guide told them to stay there and went through a door on the opposite wall. Voices could be heard through it.

"Visitors from the Underground, Joe. They wish to speak with you."

"The Underground?" The voice was weak but determined. "Alright. Let them in."

Their guide came back out and indicated for them to enter. They walked into what seemed to be a kitchen. Green wood countertops, a 80s style fridge and an oven confirmed this guess. Inside, a young woman stood with their back to them at the sink, apparently washing up. In the corner, on a simple wooden chair, sat an old man. He was probably about sixty-five, and had grey hair and a thick grey beard. His eyebrows were bushy and curled inquisitively at the group.

"Amy, is that you?" he enquired. At this, the woman turned around and stared in shock at Amy. She was about the same age but looked much older because the ends of her hair were turning grey and her face was weary and tired. She said nothing but continued to look as Amy spoke.

"Ah, yes. I've come here because I need your help." She didn't glance over the woman, Catherine if Ella recalled correctly, apparently too embarrassed to look her in the eye.

"Hmm. I see." Joe considered for a second, stroking his beard. "Is this about the Thickair?"

"Yes," Amy said, a look of surprise on her face. "How do you know about that?"

"Word travels fast here, Amy. The group have been bragging nonstop lately." He sighed and closed his eyes. "I should've known you'd be coming, actually. I imagine you'll want to find a way to stop it?"

"Why should we help you?" Catherine suddenly burst out. "You left us behind. You chose your side when you left and now you want our help now you can't handle what's happening." She looked fierce, anger evident in every line in her face. "I begged you not to go. We offered to put you up here. You could've stayed but you chose them."

"I had to go!" Amy retorted, upset. "My parents wanted me to come so badly. They would've been devastated if I'd stayed behind. What kind of life would they have had?"

"What kind of life have we had?" Joe interjected. "We stayed out of loyalty to a home that no longer existed. We've fought every day to make this work. Why should you get it easy, living in luxury down there? That place deserves to be destroyed."

Ella had had enough. She had to say something. "Look," she began. Everyone turned to look at her in surprise. "I'm with you on that. I've lived there my whole life and I hate it. It's a prison. I want to live here, in total freedom. I don't want to be controlled anymore. But the thing is, the people in it are good people. The concept was honourable once upon a time, wasn't it? It was the Leader who abandoned you, not the people. And they're really suffering. My friend and colleague Katie has a seven year old son called Sam. He's in hospital with Thickair poisoning. He's slipping away and Katie is desperate to know why. He's just a child. Did he ask to be born into the Underground? Does he have a choice in where he lives? And does he deserve to be punished for something he didn't play a part in?"

Total silence met this speech. Everyone gawked at her, open mouthed. She wished they wouldn't. She didn't like being stared at.

"You're a powerful speaker, young lady," Joe commented. This could be a negative thing to say, but his eyes shone and a faint smile was evident under his beard. He was complimenting her. "And you're right. It's the management we don't like. The innocents should not suffer as a result of their misguided actions."

He looked over at Catherine. He seemed to want to get her approval before he agreed to help. She tilted her head back, and sighed grudgingly. "OK. Yes, you have a fair point. I think we should assist in any way we can." She paused for a second, and then added, "But this to help Sam and Katie, got that? It's got nothing to do with you, Amy."

Amy looked deeply heartbroken at this, but nodded slightly. "Fine. We don't have to talk if you don't want to."

"Good. Glad we've settled that." Catherine clapped her hands briskly. "Right. Tomorrow, then, I'll take you to a contact that might be able to help you. It's a bit of a journey, and they don't like visitors, so be prepared. For now, we'll have to find you some beds. We can't have you sleeping outdoors in the summer, it's too risky."

And she led them out of the room, glaring at Amy as she went by, and went up a set of stairs Ella had missed earlier. This was getting interesting, and she loved every second of this adventure.

Thirteen

Catherine took them up the stairs and into some spare rooms on the first floor. There were two, and each were empty, the only decoration a small rectangular window. They were grubby and seemingly hadn't been cleaned in a long time, but still, Ella could just about make out the brick wall opposite.

Within ten minutes, Catherine had found the beds, and got them ready as the group watched on. There were three in the room to the left, which was to be the girl's quarters, and two in the other, which Nathan and Matt would sleep in. Catherine introduced herself properly as she worked, apparently trying to be friendly but still appearing hostile.

"I'm Catherine Parry. Joe is my father, and Amy's godfather." Amy looked up at this, but said nothing. "We used to be best friends. Our families stayed here after everyone else left, but ten years ago they decided they'd had enough and took Amy with them."

"It must be hard, living out here." Ella had noticed the tension between the two women, who were refusing to look at each other, and wanted to change the subject. "I can't imagine what it's like."

Catherine nodded. "It is hard. It wasn't too bad when everyone was here, but since the alliance crumbled, we've basically been struggling to survive. The weather is so volatile out here, it makes growing seasons hard to predict and food is sometimes hard to come by. Everyone mostly keeps to themselves and neighbours can be hard to find as everyone wants to be left alone; nobody trusts anybody anymore. I'm sure it would've been easier to give up and leave for the Underground, but that's not our way. We did this to the planet and we can't just run away from our problems. We have to face the consequences of our actions, no matter how unpleasant."

After the beds were set up, they went back downstairs to the kitchen to get some breakfast. Catherine, it turned out, was an excellent cock; it was probably the best food Ella had ever eaten. When she complimented her on this, she shrugged it off and said it was probably because the food was home-grown. They had a greenhouse area off the side of the house that they used to grow their own crops. This intrigued Ella, and while the others stayed inside to unpack, she followed Catherine into the greenhouse to help tend to the plants.

The moment she walked in she was aware of a strong smell. But it wasn't like the toxic stench of the outside. No, this smelled *good*, earthy and natural. She'd never been around any kind of plant before. Catherine smiled as she gazed around in wonder, shaking her head and laughing.

"You really don't have any kind of life down there, do you? Imagine never having seen a garden before!"

And indeed, Ella thought she had been missing out. She was unsure at first, but with Catherine's guidance, she quickly grew to love gardening. The smell of the dirt, the feel of the soft petals against her fingers… it was a sensory overload, and she realised that for twenty-one years she'd been deprived of any kind of sensation. It was all so clinical, but here there was so much colour and light, so many things to do, new places to explore. It was a beautiful kaleidoscope, messy but so worth seeing. The emotion of it almost overwhelmed her.

Then she had an idea. She ran to get her
sketchbook and pencils and returned to Catherine,
explaining she drew a little and asked if she could
draw her. She agreed. She knelt by the roses while
Ella sketched, and sometime later an image formed
on the page.

Once it was complete, she showed Catherine, who
was amazed. "That's incredible," she gushed. "You
have a gift!"

Encouraged by this, she spent the rest of the day
depicting this new world she found herself in. By four
o'clock, she had pictures of Joe, sat in his wooden
chair in the kitchen, one more of Catherine stood
at the kitchen counter, a few of the group, and even
some of the house. It was good to commit all this
detail to paper; it was a permanent reminder of this
place, both lovely and deadly, just in case she never
saw it again after she returned to the Underground.

At six o'clock they all gathered for dinner, round
the simple table in the kitchen. Their hosts found
some more chairs and they ate in silence, until
suddenly Joe spoke.

"You know, we never asked your names," he
remarked suddenly. "If you're to be our guests we
really should know what you're called."

This was true. They hadn't told them their names. It had slipped her mind earlier to do so.

Nathan spoke first. "I'm Nathan Bailey and I'm twenty years of age. I've studied the surface for a while but I've never been before."

"Matt Hurst." Matt spoke gruffly, as if he'd rather not talk at all. "I used to live on a farm on the outskirts of the city but I left at eighteen. I had to get away from the bad influences of the group."

"My name is Lacey, Lacey Montgomery." She smiled as she said this. She seemed to be eager to please, very sociable. "I'm seventeen, almost eighteen, and I was born in the Underground. I decided to challenge myself and see the wider world for the first time."

Amy didn't speak, just carried on eating miserably.

It was Ella's turn. "Well, I'm Ella. Technically it's Ella Castley but I prefer just Ella. I just turned twenty-one and I live alone, working as a librarian. It's a sad, lonely existence."

Nathan furrowed his brow at this. "You never mentioned that to me. Are you unhappy with your life, by any chance?"

She wasn't sure how to answer that. She was so used to lying about being happy, that she never considered she could tell the truth about how she felt. She thought she'd be a burden if others knew. But she couldn't very well lie to her best friend, so she decided to be honest. He did deserve to know after all they'd been through together.

"Yes, I'm unhappy. Desperately unhappy." It was a relief to say it out loud, as if getting a weight off her chest that had been dragging her down for years. "I never told you because I didn't want to worry you or drag you into my difficulties, but yes, I want more from life. Ever since Mum died, you were my only friend, and I'm incredibly grateful for that, but I needed something else. I spent five dismal years with my father but even when I struck out on my own, I was sad. I had no more family and no social circle to call on. I only had my job but that wasn't enough." She sighed heavily. "The truth is, recently I realised I wanted to live in Paris. Now it's all I can think about. I wasn't sure I could do it, but ever since I came here I've felt *free*, even happy, for the first time since I was twelve. I don't want to go back. Ever."

"I'm sorry," Nathan mumbled. He looked genuinely upset. "I should've asked, I should've been there for you. I knew it was tough for you after your mum died but I didn't know how tough. I must've been a lousy friend if you didn't feel you could confide in me."

Ella shook her head. "No, no, that's not it. I was just in a bad place and I thought I could handle it but I couldn't. Now, though, everything's different." She gave him a small smile. "Sir."

Nathan was startled but smiled back. "I'm glad to hear it, my lady."

There was a moment of silence, while everyone exchanged confused glances. Then, Catherine burst out, "That's awful. You shouldn't have to live like that, Ella. If you truly don't want to go back there, you can live here with us. You have a right to be happy and if this makes you happy, do what's right for you."

"Yes," agreed Joe. "Follow your heart. If you want to stay, just give us a shout. You'd be more than welcome."

This was extraordinarily kind. Almost too kind. She wasn't sure she deserved such kindness- but then again, could she face returning to her bleak reality in the bunker?

She didn't know.

Fourteen

As the day drew to a close, they all retired to their beds.

The sky was dark and black clouds loomed ominously in the heavens. Catherine told them this might mean a thunderstorm was coming. She didn't sound too worried- obviously this was a commonplace occurrence here- but the thought of such a thing panicked Ella.

At least she was inside, she supposed. This sure beat sleeping in a tent on the ground, even with the lumpy mattress and thin duvet. She tossed and turned for a few hours, even after Lacey and Amy had nodded off, but eventually managed to fall asleep.

She wasn't sure what time it was or how long she had been out for the count when a low rumbling sound came from the distance. She stirred sleepily, and wondered why she had woken up, when she heard it again. It was a menacing growl, like a hundred lions, and it struck fear into her. The thunderstorm was here.

It was here.

She lay in terror as the thunder drew nearer, and rain began to patter on the window. It got heavier and heavier until it was a downpour, and the thunder was right over them. Then, without warning, a flash of yellow, fleeting and blinding. Lightning.

She remembered her mother talking about these storms when she was a kid. She must have been eight or nine at the time, and was going through a phase where she had frequent nightmares. She was frightened to go to sleep. Her mother found it more and more difficult to soothe her, so one night she decided to tell her about when she was too scared to sleep through a storm.

"It was so loud," she recalled. "It was right over our house. I was a nervous child and didn't like thunderstorms anyway, but this one was the worst I'd ever encountered. The wind howled, the rain hammered at my window, and if I was about to fall asleep, I'd be woken up by the flashes of lightning. I didn't get a wink of sleep that night, and my parents had to call the school to get me a day off so I could get some rest in the morning. But I got through it, and when the next storm came, I felt braver and slept through the night."

This story might've seemed counterproductive, but it worked. She stopped fending off tiredness, trying to be brave like her mother, and eventually the nightmares stopped. Her mother had taken her to the chocolate store as a reward for being so courageous.

She was no longer a child, but right now, she felt like a scared little girl. She lay under the duvet, listening to the noises of the storm. She knew she shouldn't be worried, it couldn't harm her, but it was just so powerful that she suddenly felt small and insignificant. Nature really was in charge here, and it didn't let you forget.

The sound of the rain finally calmed her mind enough to give in to sleep, though, and she didn't wake until seven the next morning. Amy and Lacey were still slumbering either side of her, so she got up as quietly as she could and crept downstairs for breakfast.

She was greeted by a cheery Joe and Catherine. "Good morning, Ella," they said as she sat down beside them. "I hope the thunderstorm didn't keep you up."

"It wasn't too bad," she answered, as she ate gratefully. "I got used to it."

She had got used to a lot of things since she'd arrived here. But not in the negative sense that it took on in the Underground. Here, she got used to the new things she experienced, and wanted to learn more about them. She was eternally curious, thirsty for more knowledge.

Presently everyone else descended to join the trio. Their appearances varied vastly; Amy and Lacey had somehow not stirred at all last night, so they looked healthy and rested. Matt appeared as if he had slept well, but his demeanour never changed from 'grouchy' so it was hard to tell. Nathan, on the other hand, had clearly been kept awake. She could tell this by his pale face and tired eyes. He took his seat without meeting anyone's gaze; it had clearly been a rough night.

"Are you OK?" she asked, perturbed by his bad mood.

"No," he replied. "I didn't get an ounce of sleep last night. You seem to have been able to ignore that storm, but I wasn't."

He was being sarcastic. This troubled her even more. He hated sarcasm, and had told other kids off at school for it. *It's the worst form of humour,* he chastised. *It always comes at someone's expense.* He really must have been spooked.

"Hey," Matt said. "We were all scared. Ella can't have had a great night, either."

Matt coming to her defence? That wasn't what she had been expecting of him. Maybe there was another, softer, side to him after all.

It seemed to have worked, anyway, because Nathan quickly apologised. "Yes. That's true. I'm sorry, Ella. I shouldn't have snapped at you like that."

"It's fine. Really," she assured him. "I barely slept, too."

She wasn't being honest, but she didn't want to say how good her sleep really was. This concerned her just as much. She was hiding things from her best friend. They were fighting. They'd never so much as raised their voice to each other before.

They'd been like brother and sister since they were kids. Thick as thieves, joined at the hip. Now they were growing apart, or so it seemed. He clearly didn't like this place, and she loved it so much she was actually considering taking Joe and Catherine up on their offer. He was drifting away. She was losing her only friend. This gave her an agonising dilemma.

Could she really sacrifice her only hope of happiness to reconcile their friendship? Equally, could she risk losing him altogether to be herself and follow her dream? She wanted to believe their bond could survive them being in separate places, but she seriously doubted it. This felt like home to her already, but Nathan was too important to her to just brush aside.

There was an awkward silence for the rest of breakfast. She was deep in thought, weighing up the pros and cons of each option, and not getting a clear winner. She was startled out of her thoughts, however, when Catherine suddenly announced that it was time to leave.

Of course. They were going to see her contact today. They were informed that only four of them could come, so Amy volunteered to stay behind, somewhat hesitantly. The rest of the group followed Catherine outside into the warm sunshine and into the street. The heat was beating down on them relentlessly, the sun glaring. Still, the sunlight felt nice on her back, and the distant skyscrapers glimmered in the sun's rays exquisitely. She could find the beauty in this place anywhere, it seemed.

They eventually arrived at a road, and a car parked on it. This was clearly Catherine's, as she

opened it with a set of keys and got into the front
seat. Ella somehow wangled the passenger seat, while
Nathan, Matt and Lacey huddled together on the
back seat.

She'd never been in a car before. The closest thing
the Underground had was buggies, and the only
people who got to drive them were the workers in
INDUSTRY or FARMING AND AGRICULTURE.
This vehicle fascinated her- its shape, its colour, the
many buttons and appliances it had. She wondered
what they all did. Maybe Catherine would teach her
to drive if she did decide to move here.

It was clearly second nature to Catherine, as they
were soon moving down the road. Ella watched what
she did intently, but could make neither head nor
tail of what anything was. She had never properly
researched the mechanics of cars as she had never
seen any need to. She wished she had.

And they continued driving through the city,
until Ella had completely lost track of where she was.
Where they were going was anybody's guess.

Fifteen

Half an hour later, they had driven out of the city centre and into the suburbs. The smooth tarmac roads became smaller and less well maintained; the office buildings and storefronts turned into houses. Eventually, these too gave way to greenery- trees and grass and fields and the endless blue sky. A few white clouds hovered above, and the sun shone brilliantly. Birdsong filled the air and deer could be seen on the edge of a faraway wood. A rabbit hopped across the country lane in front of them.

There was nature everywhere, and it was breathtakingly beautiful. The thunderstorm last night represented the danger of it, the sheer power and control it exerted, but this- this was the gentler side Ella hadn't been told about by her teacher. This was majestic and so worthy of seeing, despite the stifling heat in the car.

After about two hours, they reached a forested area. The road became little more than a dirt path, and trees grew so close by that their branches swiped the car like fingers. *Gee*, Ella thought, *these people really don't want to be found*. Who would go to this much effort to avoid visitors?

Catherine continued for a good hour and eventually pulled up at a gate. Towering trees lined either side of the lane so that very little light filtered down through their dark green leaves. The path continued in a straight line either way, but Catherine guided them towards the gate and down a footpath.

It was a perilous journey. Brambles and stinging nettles were everywhere; at times the path faded away altogether so that they had to wade their way through thick patches of wildflowers. Bees flew too close for Ella's liking and she was relieved when Catherine stopped and indicated that they were there.

Exactly where *here* was, though, Ella couldn't fathom. It just seemed to be a simple field. Adjacent fields contained nothing but mooing black and white cows and whinnying horses. Then they opened the gate and entered, and the foliage cleared so that a building came into focus.

It wasn't a grand complex or concrete square, as she would have expected. It appeared to be a farmer's house, small and quite cute. It had a red brick exterior and brown tiled roof, and a sweet little chimney. However, on closer inspection, there were a few odd things. The windows were boarded up on the inside, and the door was not wooden as was befitting such a house, but instead was made of thick steel. There was a hatch at the top, just like the one at Joe and Catherine's place.

How odd. What could this place possibly be?

Catherine spoke in a whisper, clearly not wanting to be discovered. "This is our best hope of getting the information you seek. I know these people and they trust me, but they may not allow you entry. They don't like being disturbed, especially by strangers."

She indicated for them to stay where they were, and approached the house confidently. She knocked on the door and waited, and a moment later the hatch opened and a pair of eyes could be seen through it.

"Catherine," the person said, sounding surprised. "What are you doing here? You don't have any business with us."

"Actually, I need your help," Catherine replied. "I bring friends from the Underground and they seek information on what's been going on. You must know something, surely?"

The person considered for a second. "Even if we did, why should we share our secrets with you? You know we don't approve of fraternising with *them*."

"They don't wish to insult us. All they want is to stop the needless suffering of the innocent citizens. Too many have died and it has to end."

The other person thought carefully, then closed their eyes and nodded. "Alright. We'll help you." The hatch closed. Then the door was opened from the inside, revealing a man stood in the doorway.

Catherine called the group over. As they walked, Ella noticed little ridges on the ground, and thin metal slots. Seven of these encircled the house. Even as they approached the stranger at the door, she could just make out the silhouettes of weapons being withdrawn into the blackness beyond.

The strange man noticed Ella's perplexed face. "That is a precaution. We need to protect ourselves. There are many who would like to get their hands on our knowledge and so we must be prepared for attack." He waited for them all to gather and then continued. "I am Adam. I belong to a small collection of people who record humanity's knowledge and safeguard it here. We observe others and write down what they do and say. They don't like us doing that. We are their enemies, and they would do anything to retrieve what we have on them."

Man. Was this what people were like here? Distrustful, solitary, hiding away from their enemies? The locals here clearly led a dangerous lifestyle in a hostile world, and it made them wary of just about everyone.

And yet, this still called to her. She couldn't explain why, but she just felt it, that burning desire filling every part of her being. She wanted to be one of them.

Adam was talking again. "If you follow me, I'll lead you to our archives. There you will find the answers you're looking for."

They did as he asked, accompanying him inside. The farm house was clearly a ruse, because they walked into a metal corridor. Adam closed the door behind them and proceeded down the hallway. It twisted and turned every which way, the occasional door leading off somewhere. The place was dimly lit, strip lights like the ones in the Underground giving off a faint glow, just enough to see by. Their footsteps echoed off the walls and ceiling, and she was suddenly reminded of her nightmare. She felt a strong urge to get out of there, but fought it and carried on.

After one more turn, they reached a set of double doors. Adam opened them and gestured them into a massive library-like room. Shelves lined every wall, and all of these shelves were filled to the brim with folders and paper. This room was more brightly lit, but still there were table lamps on the countless tables that occupied the centre of the room. A few people were working at some of these tables, scribbling notes on pieces of paper with fountain pens by the light of their lamps. They barely glanced up as the group entered, so engrossed were they in their mysterious work.

Adam took them over to a shelf on the opposite wall and began rifling through the folders on display there. They all looked the same to Ella, but he clearly knew the difference, because he promptly pulled out two folders and handed them to Catherine.

"These will answer some of your questions," he explained. "This one has details on the group in question that may give you some insight into the way they work. The other might help you identify the traitor, the so-called 'fake citizen'."

"You know who they are?" Lacey asked, a look of hope flashing across her youthful face.

"No, not exactly," Adam elaborated. "We know of them, naturally, and we have a partial description, but they are clever and have avoided much of our surveillance. The only ones who know who they are for sure are the group, and we daren't go to them. They're dangerous."

This was disheartening, but still, Ella had to hope that they could identify the traitor. They divided up the folders into two groups, and Lacey, Catherine and Matt sat down at a nearby table. Nathan and Ella took a seat at a smaller adjacent one, and opened the folder. They pulled out pieces of paper and began studying them.

What would she discover, she wondered, her excitement building as she read.

Before

This young boy was intelligent. He had grown tired of the cold, regimented life he led and yearned for more. He studied books describing the surface, watched workers carefully and one night, when everything was in place, he waited until his parents were asleep and snuck out under cover of darkness.

He had been expecting a ruined wasteland. That was what his parents told him it had become ever since humans destroyed it. But what he found was the opposite. It was beautiful. Twinkling stars glimmered in a black velvet sky, the wind whistled through the trees, an owl hooted as he approached. He loved it instantly, and decided to head towards the city, which was just visible in the darkness by the glow of a few lights.

It had begun to rain by the time he reached it. At first he was worried it was the acid rain he'd heard about, but no. It was just regular rain. He turned his face upwards to the sky to catch every drop, delighting in the sensation. He explored the city for a few hours, marvelling at everything, taking in every small detail, until suddenly he became aware it was getting on. Almost dawn. He had to get back; his parents would be up in a few hours.

Regretfully, he turned away from the new wonderland he had discovered, and crept back into his bed. Over the next few days, he tried to put the experience out of his mind, but he could not. It nagged at him, begging him to return, to sneak out again. He resisted for a while, but eventually the longing got the better of him and he gave in.

He returned time and again, and it caught the attention of the locals. They never normally had visitors. At first they warned him away, but he refused, and when they realised he would not stop they befriended him. They helped him explore further, they protected him when the weather was adverse. As the years went on and he became an adult, he came to view the city as a second home and it became an obsession.

His night-time visits came to the attention of a group. They realised they could use him to get their long-awaited revenge on the Underground and those who had abandoned them. The boy was afraid of them and didn't return for several weeks, but when he did, unable to stop himself, they said they didn't wish to harm him. They just wanted him to listen to what they had to say. Reluctantly, he agreed, and they explained their plan.

He didn't know what to think. He was horrified...

Sixteen

Ella grew more and more nauseated as she read.

She and Nathan had taken the folder relating to the traitor, the 'fake citizen', and it made for disturbing reading.

They described a young boy who visited the surface from the Underground regularly. It explained that he was born there, but his heart lay with the locals, and he adored the city as if it were his home. From there, it got worse.

He had been taken by the group and manipulated into carrying out their plan. He was the 'fake citizen', hiding in plain sight. He blended into the crowd but secretly he was plotting their destruction. The group had convinced him to turn on those he loved, and bring about the end of the Underground and all who lived there. It was revenge for the broken alliance.

Another page described the boy, but it was not very helpful. He could be anybody. All they had were brief glimpses of him as an adult as he grew wary of their observation, so most of the information was based on him as a child.

What she could discern, however, was that he was smart. A genius, almost. He had managed to give away almost nothing about himself in all those years. If he had mentioned his name to anybody, they didn't have a record of it, so he was untraceable. What's more, nobody even knew what his job was, or which Sector he lived in, or any of his associates and friends. He was a ghost.

But still, something niggled at the back of Ella's mind. A spark of recognition. She *knew* this boy somehow. She had met him. It was like a picture in her mind, she knew the colours and shapes but they refused to form a clear image. It was muddled and misshapen, there and yet not there.

She had always had good instincts. Nathan reminded her of this quite often. But she had never quite mastered how to listen to them. She knew something was wrong, or she recognised somebody, but her mind just did not know how to pinpoint details. She often tried to ignore her gut instincts anyway, preferring not to think if she could help it. Thinking was dangerous.

A few minutes later, the other table had given up and had decided it was time to head back. They'd clearly not had any luck, judging by their disappointed expressions. They handed their folders back to Adam and thanked him for his assistance. Catherine indicated that they should leave.

But as the others headed off, Adam touched Ella's shoulder to hold her back. He pulled her away from the group, and turned to her, his face serious.

"I saw your reaction earlier. You know something the others don't." He said this as a statement, not a question. "Listen to me very carefully. Don't trust anybody. If they find out what you know, you'll be in grave danger. Be careful with them."

And he walked away, leaving her speechless.

"What did Adam want?" Matt enquired as she returned to the group, pretending that she wasn't utterly shocked by what he had said.

"Oh, nothing really," she said, trying be casual and offhand. "Just wishing us luck. He's interested in what we're doing."

The others seemed to buy this, but for the whole car journey home, her mind was churning. It had been an awfully strange warning, and she couldn't understand it at all. Did Adam know more than he had let on? Did he lie when he said he didn't know who the traitor was? He had been watching her, clearly, to notice that she had recognised something. But why wouldn't he just come out and say what he knew?

And what's more, he had said she might be in danger. She had heard that before and not paid much heed, but now she was really worried. There might be a threat to her and she couldn't even say who from. What had he meant by 'be careful with them'? Could her group, her new friends, not be trusted?

Even when they got back after several hours, exhausted from the long trip, she avoided Joe and Amy's questioning. She let the others handle it, and went upstairs, pretending she had a headache and needed a lie down.

Nathan came to join her after five minutes. She was glad to see him. She needed somebody she could trust right now.

"Are you OK? You've seemed a bit… spooked ever since we were reading that folder. Is something wrong?"

She knew she could trust him but Adam's voice floated into her head, warning her against telling him everything. She heeded the advice, but felt guilty for doing so.

"Yeah, yeah, I'm fine. The journey just took it out of me, and that folder upset me. The details of the traitor sickened me to my core. I can't stop thinking about how evil they must be."

Nathan's face softened, and he nodded in agreement. "They are evil. They're a monster. It's unfathomable how much damage they've caused and I'm glad you feel as strongly as I do. Don't overdo it, though. Take time to have fun and have some me time."

She smiled as he left the room, and then put her head in her hands.

This was all getting to be too much. There was too much information bombarding her brain, too many choices, too much danger. She was drifting away from Nathan and was uncertain if she could even trust those she had hoped might be her friend. It weighed heavily on her mind and she felt like she was being dragged underwater. She was flailing and screaming to get some air, but some invisible force pulled her deeper under the waves.

Dinner went by in a blur, and she quickly forgot what she had eaten. Everyone talked merrily in the lounge until it was time for bed, and Amy and Lacey tried to get her to open up but she insisted she was fine, just a bit tired. She went to sleep quickly, but it was fitful and shallow, and she woke up before everyone else for the second day in a row.

It was a beautiful morning. The temperature had cooled off a little today, and the sun was less intense. Birds chirped happily outside. She ate breakfast absent-mindedly and didn't even notice when a visitor arrived- the same man who had let them in the day they arrived. He was apparently a family friend called Kieran and often dropped by to help Joe and Catherine. He nodded at Ella and said hello but she was too preoccupied to answer. She felt bad when his face fell when met with silence, but suddenly her mouth felt heavy, too heavy to move. Her tongue would not form a word even if she had wanted to.

The others joined her a little while later, and they talked and laughed while they ate. She tried to join in but her heart was dejected, so she just sat in silence in the corner. Eventually, the conversation turned to their next move.

"We still don't have a name," Nathan was saying, "so we need to think outside the box. What do we do now?"

"I say we go to the group," Matt replied. "Not you, I mean. Me. They know me. I can say I've come back, come to my senses, and that I want to rejoin them. With time they might tell me what they know."

"No. That's too dangerous. We need to think of a better way." Amy looked appalled at Matt's suggestion. "I think we should-"

But what Amy thought, Ella would never find out. There came a knock on the door, taking everyone by surprise. Kieran volunteered to get it, and the chat resumed, but a moment later they heard a shout.

"No! Who are you? You have no right to do this!"

Seventeen

Kieran's panicked shout alarmed the group in the kitchen. Everyone immediately looked up at the staircase, worry written all over their face.

A hushed voice could be heard at the door, too faint to make out the exact words. Kieran shouted again, frightened but angry.

"No, you're not coming in. This is a private residence and you have no authority over us or them!"

"Strangers," muttered Joe, his face pale. "You need to get out of here. They'll be looking for you."

"Why would they be looking for us?" whispered Lacey. "What's going on here?"

But before Joe could answer, Kieran descended down the stairs and entered the kitchen. He looked sheepish and ashamed of himself.

"I'm so sorry, everyone." He spoke quietly, his voice trembling with apology. "I didn't want to let them in, but they forced me. You have to hide them now."

"Go," Catherine urged the group, urgency in her voice. "Out the back way. Now!"

They all stood up and started to run, but as they left the kitchen their way was blocked by a tall man in a black uniform. He glared at the group, arms folded. He had some sort of weapon in a holster at his side.

"You aren't going anywhere."

Other people came up behind him, all dressed in the same black uniform. Ella noticed a symbol on their left shoulder. It was the symbol of the Underground's four founding principles. These people were from the Underground.

But why were they here?

The man blocking their path spoke again, into a radio. "We have located the fugitives. Over."

"Fugitives?" Matt cried out. "What are you talking about?"

"Silence," a woman at the back commanded. "You are in our custody now."

"No." Ella was confused but she wasn't going without a fight. "We aren't doing anything until you tell us who are you and what you're doing here!"

"Very well," the woman said. "We are from the Underground. Three days ago we got word that five people had gone missing from their rooms. We were concerned for your wellbeing so we tracked you here. You are going to be returned back to the Underground and questioned about why you left."

"No they are not." Joe was walking out to join them now. He looked utterly furious. "You aren't concerned for their wellbeing. You want them back so you can keep them under your control. Well, these people left of their free will, which is their right as per the Peace Agreement, and we intend to give them shelter until they decide to return of their own volition."

The guards, or whatever they were, looked surprised by Joe's outburst, but did not back off. "You are wrong there. The Peace Agreement only stood while we were co-operating. Since you renounced our help it has no legal standing. Therefore the fugitives have no right to leave and are under our custody."

Catherine walked out now, her worn face alight with rage. "The Peace Agreement still stands. We didn't renounce you first. You cut us off and left us behind. You are the ones who broke the alliance and so we are not to blame for what happened. If it is no longer law, it's because you decided that we weren't good enough."

Ella had never heard of the Peace Agreement in her life. Was that something to do with the broken alliance Nathan told her about? She suddenly realised how little she truly knew about the place she had called home for so long.

"Be that is it may, the citizens of the Underground are under our jurisdiction. They follow our rules and you follow yours. Mixing is forbidden." The woman at the back frowned but said nothing. "You were foolish to extend your support. You should not have helped them."

And the guards told them to gather their belongings and leave.

Sensing that it was hopeless, they complied. They went upstairs to get their bags, under the watchful gaze of the guards, and then were tugged out by their arms, up the stairs. Before they were pulled out the door, Ella yelled out to Joe, Catherine and Kieran, who were stood at the foot of the staircase watching disapprovingly.

"Thank you for everything! If I could've stayed, I would."

Then the door slammed shut and they were
outside. The guards told them to put their masks on
and frogmarched them out the alley and through the
empty streets. After an hour they reached the edge
of the city, and thirty minutes after that they were in
the lift, descending back down into the Underground.

Once they were inside, Ella's escort loosened her
grip on Ella's arm. It was the woman at the back who
had frowned. She couldn't understand it. Why would
she be nice to her if she was dragging her back here?

But then the lift arrived and they were pulled out.
Through the decontamination chamber, past the
check-in room, and down the escape passage. The
sight of it made Ella deeply sad. She didn't want to be
here. Now she knew with absolute certainty that she
wanted to live on the surface with Joe and Catherine.
She hated these guards for shattering that dream.

Once into the main corridor, they didn't go north,
towards the cafeteria. Instead, the guards put in the
code for Sector One and tugged them inside.

She hadn't been here in five years, but she
still knew it inside out. They walked through the
accommodation, each turn as familiar as it had been
when she was seventeen. There was the cafeteria, and
the private library with the office spaces. It was as if

she had never left.

The others, however, had clearly never been here before. They stared at everything, wondering at all the luxury here. They looked confused as they went through a door at the end of the cafeteria and down a small passage, but Ella knew exactly where they were. The guards didn't want them seen in public, so they had chosen to take the private route to MANAGEMENT, through the secret passageway Sector One had that connected to it. It had been built so the Leader and senior management could get to work without being bothered by the public, but Ella knew that it was sometimes used to bring criminals and other people to court or interrogation without the public knowing.

And as expected, they came out into management. She had been here before with her father and recognised it, but most of the citizens only knew it as the place behind the locked door where the Leader worked. It hadn't changed at all since she had last seen it. People working at desks on their computers, a few of them talking at the water cooler, and beyond, a corridor through which you could enter private offices. Megan's was much further down, out of sight, and guarded. Her father's was on the left side. She remembered it being small and somewhat dinghy. Not much more than a box.

The guards started to guide them down the corridor, towards where Ella knew interrogation was. They stopped abruptly, however, when someone called out her name. It was the same voice she thought she had recognised over the speaker, and now, stood in front of her, she knew who it was. Her heart sank like a stone.

"Eleanor, is that you?"

She sighed and closed her eyes. "It's Ella, Dad, not Eleanor. And it's good to see you too."

Eighteen

She hadn't seen him in five years, but now, here he was. Her father, Thomas Castley. He was still as pale and thin as he had ever been, his black hair neatly combed as always. He looked at her, his pale green eyes showing that he was perplexed.

"Eleanor, what are you doing here?" His focus shifted to her escort. The woman looked awkward and let go of her arm quickly. "Why are you taking my daughter to interrogation, may I ask?"

"She's one of the five fugitives we've been searching for," the man at the front answered. He had a tight grip on Matt's arm, who was looking decidedly affronted. "You remember. They snuck out in the night."

"Yes, I remember. What I don't recall is being told my Eleanor was among them." Ella was amazed.

When she had been living with him, he barely paid her any heed at all, burying himself in his work. Now, though, he was defending her angrily, as if they had always had a relationship. She didn't even really mind him calling her Eleanor. "Come to think of it, I don't recall being told you were looking for them. You know you have no right to arrest them, don't you? The Peace Agreement does still stand, whether you like it or not."

Nathan turned to look at her, and she shrugged. She had no idea what was going on but she'd take it.

"Opinions vary on that matter, Thomas. Megan gave us authorisation to arrest them. She seems to think the agreement ended the day the alliance did, and the Leader's word is the one that counts around here."

Of course her word was the most important. It wasn't like she was corrupt or anything.

"The alliance didn't 'end'. We broke it off. And if we're at fault, then we have a duty to honour any deal we made. Isn't one of the four founding principles friendship? Didn't that originally mean we helped each other, and didn't abandon anyone on their own?"

She was starting to think she may have misjudged her father. He spoke as passionately on the local's rights as they did and she respected him for that.

"Times change, Thomas. That was twenty-one years ago. Now, Megan says the fugitives are to be interrogated, and your daughter is one of them. Now, please move aside so we can do our jobs."

The guards pulled them forward, down the corridor. Her father stared, aghast, as Ella's escort accompanied her, her hand on Ella's shoulder but not pushing her. She smiled at her father as she walked by and whispered 'thank you'. She may not have talked to him since she was seventeen but she knew in that moment that she missed him.

They walked past Megan's office, and the guards stationed outside. They turned left and then right, and went through a secured door. This was interrogation, she knew that from what her father had told her, but she'd never been inside before. It was dark here, the lights overhead dimmed. Each of the guards took their charge into a room. Her escort motioned for her to enter one such room at the end of the corridor. Ella did, thankful for her kindness, and found herself in a small square room. It wasn't made of white stone, like everything else here. The walls were lined with grey metal and a single bulb light shone on the ceiling. A camera on the wall watched

as she took a seat at a wooden table in the centre of
the room. The guard sat opposite her.

"The interrogation of Eleanor Castley, on
Wednesday the 27th of July, commencing at seven
forty one am." The woman took a moment to think.
"I'm sorry about all that earlier. We were told to
be heavy-handed, but I regret that we had to use
such force."

A moment of silence, then she spoke again. "For
the purposes of this interrogation, I have to ask you
to only speak when I ask you something. I wouldn't
put you in this position if I didn't have to, but there
are rules I have to follow. As it is I'm taking a risk by
being lenient on you. I also require you to answer
truthfully and to the best of your ability. If you're
unsure of something, just ask."

"OK." This was unusual, but she was going along
with it. She was being shown some mercy and she
wouldn't argue with that.

"Do you prefer Ella or Eleanor? You seemed upset
when Thomas called you Eleanor."

"I go by Ella, but either is fine. I just don't get on
with him, that's all."

"I'll call you Ella." There was some paper and a
pen on the table, on which she was making notes.

Ella watched her curiously. "Alright then. First things first. Can you tell me why you all decided to leave in the first place?"

She wasn't sure how to answer this. Her response had to match up to the others, and they hadn't discussed what to say in the event of capture. She decided to be truthful. They would probably be, too, and she wanted to tell the truth now anyway.

"We left because there's a threat to the Underground. Nathan and Amy informed me that they had discovered a traitor was living amongst us. They put Thickair into the pumps, deleted any CCTV evidence and now have control of where it goes. They belong to a group on the surface who have plotted this for years and used him to get their revenge on us. He'd been leaving at night for years so they knew they could convince him to do as they asked. We also believe they have an accomplice, one in a position of power, who covers their tracks. That's why we didn't risk coming to you, in case their accomplice discovered we were onto them. We wanted to identify the traitor ourselves."

At this the woman looked alarmed, scribbling all that down hurriedly. "That would explain why we haven't got anywhere with our investigation. If there's an insider in management, they would want to throw us off the scent. I can see why you thought it best to investigate this yourselves." Ella was relieved that she believed her. After all, she'd taken some persuading to come along herself. "I don't suppose you have a name, do you?"

"Unfortunately not. We really tried but the traitor's good. Nobody knows anything about them. We can't identify them unless we go direct to the group responsible, and they're very dangerous."

She didn't say anything about her suspicion that she *knew* the traitor. She would sound crazy if she did; they might even accuse her of it. No, that was best kept secret.

"Oh. OK. Any identifying features, then? Or even a name for their accomplice? If they're behind this we need to apprehend them immediately."

"Yes. I know. The traitor is smart, really smart. They must be well-placed to do this, and they are quite young. Probably about my age, no older. Their accomplice... well, we had a theory, but we can't say for sure. It might be anyone here with access to the IT systems."

The woman nodded. As she read back what she had written, she suddenly realised what Ella was trying to say. She scrawled the word 'Megan' on her hand, in small letters, and looked at Ella.

"That's very helpful. Thank you." She stacked the papers into a neat pile. "That's all for today. We'll look into this matter from here. Trust us." And Ella did. She did trust this woman, whoever she was, to deal with it. "For now, then, I'd like you to stay away from the others in your group. Keep your head down. And don't go anywhere, please. I know it's hard for you, I could see how much you loved the surface, but don't go back there. At least, not for now."

She stood up, indicating for Ella to do the same. She did, following her out the room. Lacey, too, was leaving with her guard, and they shared a quick glance before looking away. As they proceeded down the corridor, Ella's escort suddenly spoke again.

"I know it's not any of my business, but it seems to me that Thomas wanted to reconnect with you. I know what happened and I know why- he can be a bit cold, I get it- but he's a good guy. Your mother would want you to try, I'm sure. He's the only family you've got."

Ella considered this statement. She was right, of course, but it had been so long. She wasn't sure she could face losing someone again.

Nineteen

*O*ver the next two weeks, Ella kept to herself. She rarely left her room except to eat, and even when she was informed she could see Nathan and the others again, she didn't.

Things had really changed in the Underground since the interrogation. Megan had been arrested and placed in Sector Five, and just like that, the mood in the place lifted considerably. The Thickair poisonings had stopped and the afflicted were slowly recovering under the guidance of doctors. There was a sense of jubilation and excitement in the air; often at night celebratory parties had to be dispersed. But even with all this joy around her, Ella was unhappy.

Her life had gone back to normal. Katie welcomed her back to her job in the library, and cheerfully informed her that Sam was out of hospital. He hadn't got off scot-free, he now had lung damage as a result of his illness that gave him difficulty breathing, but he was mostly healthy. He just couldn't do any physical activity at school anymore. A lot of people had come off much worse. Almost two hundred had died, and almost a thousand had been ill at one point.

Katie was overjoyed that it had stopped, but Ella felt nothing. Not even triumph at Megan's arrest. Her life was just as boring as it had been before. This was the dreary reality she had sought to escape, but it seemed she was now trapped in it forever. Her colleagues didn't understand and asked why she was blue when she had helped save countless lives. She didn't know how to answer.

There were still questions nagging at her, too. Megan kept protesting her innocence. At first Ella doubted the truthfulness of her claims, but over time she began to wonder if an innocent woman really was in jail. Furthermore, they still hadn't identified the traitor, the fake citizen. The new Leader, Vicky White, was being guarded closely to prevent them brainwashing her too, but still the thought of someone still being out there troubled Ella. She still thought she knew them, but frustratingly, she could not come up with a name.

To add to her woes, her father kept sending her letters begging her to meet up with him. She felt bad for ignoring them, she really did want to catch up, but she just felt scared. Her mother had wanted nothing to do with him after the divorce, she opted to raise Ella on her own, but she never explicitly said to Ella never to talk to him again. Perhaps her interrogator had been correct. Perhaps she owed it to her mother, and to her father, to try.

One day she ran into him in the main cafeteria. They ate together and talked for about twenty minutes, but it did not help her decide. He asked why she hadn't talked to him since she moved out and the question upset her. Why did that matter?

"I didn't think you wanted to talk to me either. You didn't try to find me. And anyway, I was loyal to Mum. I thought she would've wanted me to live my life without you."

"I did try to find you. Believe me, I did. I asked everywhere but nobody knew where you were. All I had was Sector Four. You could've been anywhere in there. It was no good." He rubbed his eyes as if he was tired. "And I know you and Mum were close. I expected you to be, after she told me to go away. I don't know if she told you this, but even then I wanted to see you. I begged to see you even once. I think she was just too angry after we split to forgive me. It was my fault; I was a fool to put work over my family. It cost me Mum, and it cost me you. But I wish you would've tried. Didn't you miss me?"

And then he told her he had to get to work, and that he would like to see her again. She said goodbye and watched him disappear through the door to MANAGEMENT, her mind swirling.

To take her mind off things, she took to looking at her drawings of the surface. She was glad she'd done them, because they gave her comfort. Her favourite was the one of Catherine in the greenhouse, tending to the roses. It evoked memories of that wonderful place, the wonderful earthy smell of the dirt on her fingers, the soft touch of the leaves against her skin. In an attempt to recreate this sensation, she bought a few houseplants, but it wasn't the same. She longed for that greenhouse, and its owners. The longing drove her mad.

A month after they returned, she finally decided to get out of her room and talk to someone. She arranged to meet Nathan in the communal area, and was delighted to see Leanne and Naomi Foster there too. The four of them spent a delightful afternoon talking.

"It's so good to finally catch up, Ella," Naomi said. "I still think about our play dates. I was so upset when they stopped."

"So was I," she replied. "That was when my life began to spiral out of control. I had lost Mum and Dad didn't seem to really care, and all my friends turned on me. Nathan here was the only one who stood by me. He kept me sane all these years."

"That's good," Leanne noted. "I'm thankful you had a friend like him."

Nathan brushed off this praise. "Ella's helped me a lot too. I know it hasn't been easy for her over the last nine years, and especially now I know it's tough. You wanted to stay up there, didn't you? But you have kept me steady, too. You've listened to my geeky ramblings and stood up for me, and I wouldn't have lasted past that thunderstorm if it wasn't for you."

"It's that bad up there, huh?" Naomi asked.

"Yeah," Ella said. "It's as bad as Mum said, but it's also as beautiful as she said. It's intoxicating, the beauty and danger all rolled into one. We went there to find the traitor, but it became like home to me."

"It must be hard for you," soothed Leanne. "You don't seem happy here. And after all that, you didn't even get enough time up there to identify the traitor, whoever they are. It must've been a blow."

"Have they got any ideas about that?" Naomi piped up. "I mean, they must have some idea of who it is."

"No, not yet. They're trying, but the traitor's intelligent. Megan won't say, so we're getting nowhere."

Nathan said this casually. It was an unremarkable comment, but it got her thinking. Again, that blurred picture came into mind, refusing to yield its secret. After they had said goodbye and parted ways, even as she lay staring at the white stone ceiling, she couldn't stop thinking about that image, muddled and ever-present.

She thought about what she knew about the traitor. They were smart. They were well-placed. They loved the surface and knew it well. Adam had warned her about the group- but what if he'd recognised just one of them? What if he'd recognised the traitor, and he knew that she knew, and he wasn't referring to all of them, just that one person? But in that case, who in her group was the fake citizen, given the very specific details of the person who visited the surface at night?

And then she realised she knew exactly who. The picture came into focus, each colour and shape moving to form a face, a face she knew all too well. She could hardly breathe. This couldn't be true.

The image in her head was of Nathan. She wanted to dismiss it, to believe it to be false, but every instinct in her body told her it was true. He'd done this. Megan was never involved, she was simply the scapegoat. The obvious suspect. He worked with the IT on the pumps. He could've manipulated where the Thickair went. He could've put it in. He probably knew she'd believe anything he told her, he played on her dislike of Megan Masters and used that to get her to come. And of course, he would want her to go. He knew she suspected something; it was only a matter of time before she arrived at him. He had to bring her along to watch what she was told, to monitor what she knew and so he would know when she was suspecting him. That was why he'd come to her after Adam warned her, pretending to be concerned but really wanting to throw her off the scent.

No. No. This was impossible. This...

She was dizzy. She staggered around, her mind heavy and slow. She only just had time to realise she was being gassed when she collapsed onto the ground. She fought it off for a few seconds before her eyes closed and she fell asleep.

Before

he group's plan sickened the boy. He told them they could forget it, he'd never turn on those he held dear. But they told him of their suffering, and he was moved.

They said they'd struggled every day to make it out here since the alliance crumbled. Since the Underground turned their backs on their plight. They fought against the elements, against each other, against incredible odds, and they'd been made resilient but also angry. How could they suffer so and the citizens of that bunker get it easy? How could they live in luxury, in comfort, and forget about those they had left behind?

Their argument was powerful and the boy promised to think about it. And the more he did, he got more and more enraged. He looked at e-posters of the four founding principles and realised they were lies. They were tools management used to control

the population, their honourable meaning long
since forgotten. Even his parents had told him lies,
encouraged by the Leader. And he made his decision.

He returned to the group and told them he
was on board. He told them he could do it easily,
he was well-placed in his job and clever enough to
avoid suspicion. He'd blame the Leader and pretend
to want to help. The group were pleased and got
everything in place, and on the night of Thursday the
16th of June, he carried out their plan.

At midnight, when everyone was asleep, he
crept out his room as he had done so many times
before. Now, though, he was headed towards
INFRASTRUCTURE. He entered his workplace with
the usual code, and walked towards the pumps. He
knew how to open them. The hatch opened and for
a moment, he hesitated. Then he opened the jar of
swirling grey Thickair and poured it in like water,
smirking as he did. He closed the hatch and went
to his office, logging into the computer station. He
modified the air quality report so that it seemed that
there *was* no Thickair, and tweaked the system so
that he alone was in control of where it went.

He then crept back to his room, but he
accidentally slammed his door on the way in. He

hoped no-one had heard. Then he went to bed, and lay smiling at the ceiling. It was done. He had exacted revenge on behalf of his friends.

He was not scared. He was in danger himself, of course, if the Thickair got out of control, but this did not bother him. If he fell ill, he'd done his job. That was what mattered.

It had begun. He was in control. He was powerful.

He was Nathan Bailey…

Twenty

She woke up in what appeared to be some sort of engine room.

She groaned groggily, and slowly opened her eyes to see someone kneeling in front of her. It was Nathan. He smiled as she came to.

"Wakey wakey, Ella," he said, smirking.

She felt a surge of hot anger and moved to lunge forward, but her hands were tied behind her back. She glared fiercely at her former best friend but said nothing.

Next to her, Lacey and Matt were also coming to, their hands tied behind their back as well. They stared around in horror, confused, but Ella knew exactly what was happening.

"Nice to see you all again. Sorry about all this, but this is strictly necessary, I assure you. Can't have you running off to tell anyone, can I?"

"It was you," Matt spat, hatred filling his every word. "It was never Megan. It was you."

Lacey gasped, tears spilling down her cheeks.

"Yes. I was the traitor. I did this. And I almost succeeded, if it hadn't been for those pesky guards. I wasn't expecting them to find us."

"I should've seen it from the start," mumbled Ella. "I should've known you for what you really were. A fraud."

"Yes, you should have," Nathan agreed. "All the signs were there. I knew you suspected something, but I didn't know how little you really *knew*. It was easy to fool you, all of you. It was easy to take you along for a ride. Honestly, Megan Masters indeed. Why on Earth would she do this?"

"Why would you?" Ella's anger was rising and falling like waves, melancholy always waiting to take over. "There was no reason for you to do this, either. I understand your anger but taking it out on innocents is not the answer."

"Maybe not, but it achieves something. It gets the management to wake up. It lets them know what we're capable of."

"Where's Amy?" Lacey suddenly burst out. "Is she hurt?"

Nathan laughed, a callous, cold, unfeeling laugh. "You really don't know where she is? Wow. You really don't have this all figured out. I thought you did, at least, Ella."

She hadn't thought about Amy. Hadn't noticed her absence. But now the reason why she wasn't here became clear. Before she could speak, though, a voice came over the speaker.

"Attention, everyone." It was Amy. *It was Amy.* "I have important news for you. The Underground has been taken over by us. We have imprisoned Vicky White and her management team, and we are in charge. We are a group called Those Left Behind, and we are from the surface."

Ella looked at Nathan in horror. He simply laughed in response. "You see? It's so easy to fool you. What did you really know about Amy? What did she tell you about herself? You were trusting fools, all of you."

"Those Left Behind have a mission to destroy the Underground," Amy continued. "The Thickair attacks were not random or unlucky. We were responsible. We determined who fell ill and who didn't." A pause. Then, "We want to punish those who broke the alliance with the surface and abandoned them on their own. They have suffered needlessly, and we wish to bring a taste of that pain to you. This was the only way management would listen to us."

Ella didn't know where she was, but she could just faintly hear sounds of people shouting in the distance. They were panicked screams; children were crying. It was madness. How could Nathan and Amy do this to them?

"I say this not to frighten you but to offer you a hope of escape." Amy was speaking louder and with more authority in her voice. "We have failed to destroy this place in our first attempt, so we have decided to make you a deal. If you leave with us for the surface, you will be spared. If you stay here, you will not. We are not bluffing. We have three prisoners who threatened to betray us already. We will destroy this place in three hours. The exit has been left open for you to leave. It is the cleaning cupboard by Sector One. I trust you will make the right decision."

The speaker cut out. Nathan nodded approvingly. "Good. That's done." He stood up and walked to the door. "Any final questions before I leave?"

"Why is Amy helping you?" Lacey sobbed. "What did you do to her?"

"I didn't do anything to her. She was a spy sent here ten years ago to keep an eye on management.

She works there. She saw the footage of me and knew who I was immediately. She deleted it and came to me to offer help. I was not aware there were any spies here but I was grateful for her assistance. She's been most useful." He put his hand on the door handle and twisted it open. "And now it's time for me to leave. Have fun."

He closed the door behind him and locked it.

That was it. Game over.

Lacey was sobbing quietly. Ella just felt numb. Nathan had betrayed her. Her oldest friend. Was he visiting the surface when they became friends? Was he plotting his revenge while talking to her at breakfast?

"I can't believe him," Matt snarled. "We trusted him and he did this to us."

"What are they going to do? How they going to destroy this place?" sniffed Lacey.

"Explosives," said Ella. She didn't know how she knew, but her gut told her they had explosives. "They've rigged the entire Underground up with them. In three hours, his computer will set them off. By that time he, Amy and half the population will have made it out."

"And the other half?" Matt asked, but he looked as if he knew the answer.

"They won't have their revenge if everyone gets out, will they?" Ella replied. "That's why it's only three hours. So that enough will make it out to repopulate the city, but not enough so that they're robbed of their final vengeance."

She looked at her watch. Four thirty pm. By seven thirty, it would be all over.

But she couldn't sit helplessly by and do nothing. She thought of her father. If Amy had truly imprisoned the management, her father would be among them. She had to do something. As she moved to stand up, a rope came loose on her ties. She fumbled for it, and began trying to unknot it behind her back.

"Ella, stop. It's hopeless." But Matt's pessimism did not put her off, and after some effort, she succeeded in releasing the knot. She went over to Matt and Lacey and untied them, too, then went over to the door. Locked, but surely she could pick it.

"Anyone got anything sharp?" she asked. They fumbled around in their pockets, and Lacey found a hairpin. It worked. After some trial and error, she finally got the door open. Thank goodness it had been a keyhole and not a keypad. Nathan hadn't accounted for that.

If he hadn't accounted for that, what else hadn't he accounted for? Maybe they could switch off the explosives by getting to his computer. All they had to do was find it.

"Ready?" Ella asked. Matt and Lacey nodded, and they set off in search of Nathan's office.

Twenty-one

"*Where are we?*" *Matt said, as he stared around at the corridor that they found themselves in.*

"Infrastructure," Lacey replied. Her face was red from crying but her voice had stopped trembling; she seemed determined to do this. Ella respected her courage, given she was only seventeen. "That must have been the boiler room. There's the entrance to the pumps and pipe systems over there, look." She pointed to the left, and as she said, there was a door at the end of the corridor. It was dark in here, but there was just enough light to see by because one strip light had been left on. It was kind of eerie here, but she pushed aside her fear. It would do her no good now.

"Which way do we go, then?" Ella asked. "Do you know where his office might be?"

Lacey pondered. "Well, Infrastructure workers have their offices here, I know that. I know where they are, but which one is his is anyone's guess. Plus, we need to know his code to get in."

"I might have some ideas." They had been friends since childhood. She knew practically everything about him, and she was sure his code would be something memorable. She could try.

"Right. Let's go, then." The two women started to walk off, but Matt stayed where he was.

"I don't think we should all go." His voice was resolute and strong, his face set. "You two go ahead; you're best equipped to stop the explosives. I'll find the management and let them know what's going on."

"But Matt, what if Amy's still there?" Lacey cried out. "She might be armed... you could be seriously hurt!"

"I know. But it gives you a chance." He smiled, probably for the first time since she had met him. "I'll take that risk if it helps you."

Ella felt a surge of gratitude. She ran to hug him. He might be surly and a bit distant, they might not have got off on the right foot, but he was, deep down, a good person. She could finally see that.

"Go," Matt urged. "Do it."

Ella nodded, then ran in the opposite direction, Lacey following close behind. She told them to take a right turn, and then go straight ahead. She followed Lacey's instructions, her heart beating like a drum as she hastened towards the offices.

Run, Ella. Seek...

Her mother's voice popped into her head, uttering the same words she had done in her nightmare, so long ago. This time, though, they didn't feel like a warning, or a bad omen. No, they were words of encouragement. She felt her mother beside her, telling her to go on, to fight.

I will, Mum. I promise. I won't let you down.
Dad needs me.

"We're almost there!" shouted Lacey. They turned a corner and there were the offices. She saw the problem immediately. There must have been almost a hundred of them, and each was hidden behind an identical door. How could they ever find Nathan's?

"Any ideas?" Lacey asked.

But before she could answer, a voice rang out, loud and booming in the total silence. It was him. He was here.

"Well, well. I should've known."

He stepped out into the dim light, no longer smirking but still looking amused. Contempt rose within her, an overpowering wave of emotion that she could no longer control. She seethed at the sight of him, his smug face, and his callous indifference. He seemed deaf to the desperate wails of families in the distance.

"You." She said this slowly, deliberately, venom in every note. "What are you doing here, traitor?"

"I thought you might try to escape," Nathan said casually, wandering aimlessly around the room. "I knew you wouldn't just give up. I thought I'd let you try. I'm surprised you came here, though. Didn't you think I'd be waiting?"

"You're so arrogant." Lacey said this, detest evident in her eyes. "You think you're so smart. You think you're better than us all, don't you? That you have a right to do anything you want and that there'll be no consequences. Well, newsflash, you don't. So get out of the way or I'll make you."

Nathan actually laughed at this, a high cold laugh. "You think you can stop this? Stop me? Does Matt think he'll succeed in finding the management? They can't do anything about this, it's too late now. It's begun."

"You lied," Ella whispered. She felt queasy; the room spun around her. "You never wanted anyone to get out, did you? The three hours was a trick. That was to get everyone panicked and awake before you set the explosives off. To punish them *properly*."

"Well done." He said this in a patronising manner, as if he was speaking to a baby. She resisted the urge to slap him. "Our plan was never to repopulate the surface. It's too far gone. Amy and I never intended to get out in time. All we wanted was to teach you all a lesson, to give you a taste of the pain they've felt all these years. They'll be the last of the human race. With the weather up there, we'll be extinct in a few years."

What madness had taken hold of him? What delusion had its grip on his mind that he thought *this* was the answer? She suddenly saw him for what he truly was, and he repulsed her.

But what if it wasn't too late? What if he could be persuaded to do the right thing?

"You don't have to do this," she said, in a pleading voice. Lacey looked at her in surprise. "This can still be stopped. This isn't the way. Let everyone go and we'll discuss it. Nothing is ever too far gone. Not the surface, and not you."

Lacey suddenly saw what she was doing, and joined in. "Yes. Help us. You said this achieves something. It lets us know what you're capable of. If you're capable of this, you're capable of helping us save them. They're good people, all of them. Do they deserve this?"

Nathan listened, unmoved. "We've cheated our fate for too long. We should've let nature do its job twenty-one years ago. We did this to the world, our greedy ignorant ancestors, and building this place was a way to escape our punishment, postpone our judgement. We've subjugated each other and left friends to suffer- for what? Friendship? Trust? Democracy? Hard work? Those four words are lies. They never meant anything. The right thing to do is to stop hiding and face the music. This isn't living, either here or on the surface. This is beyond repair. We're better off not being here at all."

Ella was dumbfounded. He was clearly ill, mad. He couldn't be reasoned with. He was right on some things, but destroying humanity could not solve the problem.

"And now, I think it's time for us to bow out, don't you?"

"What?"

Nathan reached into his pocket and drew out a weapon. A gun. It was small but terrifying, the black O-shaped barrel facing towards the two women. He jerked his head sideways and grinned, maniacally.

"Say goodbye, my ladies."

But then there came the sound of people running down the corridor. A group of people rushed towards them- Matt, and her father, and a few guards in tow. Nathan looked shocked as they approached him, and pointed the gun towards them, but then he fell to the ground, convulsing. The guards had fired a taser at him. They dragged him off the ground by his arms, still twisting in pain, and she rushed to embrace her father in relief.

Twenty-two

She threw her arms around him, sobbing into his shoulder unrestrainedly. He whispered 'it's OK' into her ear, and in that moment she forgave him for everything.

"I'm so glad you're fine," she sniffed. "I was so worried about you."

"How did you find us?" Lacey asked, her voice shaking but no longer emotional. "Did Matt send you here?"

"Actually, no," one of the guards replied. It was the woman who had interrogated Ella. She beamed happily as father and daughter embraced. "We had a little outside help. Although Matt told us where to find you, of course, and to hurry."

"Who-?" Ella began to ask, but she was shocked by the answer she got. A woman stepped out from the back of the group, watching Nathan be handcuffed and dragged away.

"Hi, guys," Amy said, somewhat sheepishly. Ella released her father and approached her, shocked. "I'm sorry for all that. I didn't want to drag you into this, but he insisted."

And Ella completely understood.

"You were never a spy for them, were you?" She saw it all now. It was so obvious. "You came here because you thought the group would do a stunt like this. And when Nathan put the Thickair in, you pretended to be a spy wanting to help him, but in reality you were passing information to management to apprehend him."

Lacey stood open-mouthed. Clearly she hadn't seen this coming.

"That's right. I know Matt from the old days and he told me that the group were concocting a plan." She nodded at Matt. "He knew I was here to stop any such attack, and told me to keep an eye out. So when my colleague saw the CCTV, and showed it to me, I decided the best way to stop Nathan was to pretend to be on his side. I told him the footage had been deleted and that I would use my position to cover his tracks. I hoped he would slip up and say something incriminating."

"But then he offered Amy something better," Matt continued. "He said we ought to go to the surface under the guise of wanting to help, and that we should invite some others to make it look more legit. Amy didn't want to put anyone else in danger, but in order to maintain his trust, she agreed. Amy suggested me, knowing my connections would be a good disguise for our true intentions. Lacey heard about it and volunteered, and we couldn't tell her the truth, so we let her come but vowed to protect her at all costs."

"And me?"

"That was Nathan's idea, I'm afraid," Amy responded. "He knew you suspected something was up, and wanted to keep an eye on you. I couldn't blow my cover so I said that would be a great idea, you could be a threat, but really I hoped you might figure it out using your infamous instincts. And you did, but a little later than I'd hoped. You were now in grave danger because Nathan saw Adam warn you. I called my colleagues to come in and 'arrest' us so he wouldn't harm you. I wanted to arrest him there and then; we had all the proof we needed. But he violated orders to come visit me one night. He wanted to up the stakes. Place explosives around the Underground and destroy it. He beseeched me to go along with it, to go down with the ship, as it were."

"It was too good an opportunity to pass up." Her father was speaking now, his hand on Ella's shoulder. "We told Amy to agree. He trusted her with the placing of the explosives, and he would gas you three and kidnap you. But Amy never placed the explosives. There never was a threat to anyone. Matt knew about the gas but if he told you two, you might panic and accidentally reveal everything. I felt awful letting you be kidnapped and threatened by him. Believe me. But it had to be done, or we wouldn't have what we needed to arrest that maniac."

"I know." Ella turned to look at him and smiled. "I know you'd never place me in any harm if it wasn't for the greater good. And I know you'd do everything in your power to make sure he didn't get his way."

"After the kidnappings, we were ready and waiting. We weren't expecting to see Matt. He was panicked. He told us you were going to his office to defuse the explosives and we had to hurry. If *he* caught you he'd be a real threat."

"I should've told you. After you picked the lock." Matt looked ashamed of himself. "I should never have put you in danger. These guys were more than capable of handling it. I only thought he might've bugged the room, and run before we caught him. I'm sorry."

Lacey suddenly protested. "No. Don't blame yourself. You did the best you could. You came to save us. If you'd told us, we'd probably have gone anyway just to tell Nathan what we thought of him. I would have, anyway."

"So would I," agreed Ella. "Even if you'd told me and Lacey everything, I would've been so angry with Nathan at causing me to doubt my friends that I would've confronted him myself. So you did us a favour. We were all in the dark and it might well have given you enough time to come to us."

"Doesn't make me feel any better, though."

"You're a good person, Matt," Ella asserted. "You care about our wellbeing. I might not have seen it from the beginning but you were always there protecting us."

"I agree," her father said. "But next time, Eleanor, please don't put yourself in unnecessary danger, got it? I can't lose you again."

"Hopefully there won't be a next time," she grinned. "And I can't lose you, either. Mum wouldn't want that."

A distant scream startled them all. The crowds still thought they were in danger.

"Oh no. I totally forgot."

"Its fine, Amy," Ella assured her. "They'll understand once we explain."

They all headed off out of INFRASTRUCTURE and into the neighbouring MANAGEMENT. There, they headed into the Leader's office, where the speaker was, and called for everyone to stop panicking, the situation was under control and the culprits apprehended. *That's all they need to know for now*, her father told them.

Being in this office raised another question for Ella. "Hey, can I ask you something? If you knew he was trying to pin it on Megan all along, where is she? You didn't actually imprison her, did you?"

"Oh no. We just told everyone we did," her father clarified. "For her public appearances of pleading innocence, we just took her to a cell in Sector Five for the purposes of filming. She's been keeping her head down in her room most of the time. She was in on our investigation into Nathan from the beginning, so she knew she had to take the fall, at least temporarily, and she agreed. If anyone else was suspected Nathan's plan would fall to pieces and he'd leg it to the surface before we could get to him. Vicky White was never truly Leader. Megan ran the show from behind the scenes. She's done very well."

"I want to meet her," Ella said. "If I can, that is. I want to apologise to her for blaming her all along."

"Of course, if you want to."

Her father and Amy went to take her to Megan's room in Sector One. She was still a fairy-tale princess to look at, but suddenly that didn't matter anymore. They had a long and riveting conversation, where Ella said she was sorry for thinking she was evil and not liking her before that, and Megan smiled and said it was fine, that was the plan. She thanked Ella and her new friends for doing their bit to save the Underground and promised to thank them properly soon with an award or medal or something like that.

And as Ella left the not-so-bad-after-all Leader to have a lie down in her own room, she thought about everything she had learned over the past few weeks and realised that while her life still wasn't perfect, it was worth living for sure.

After

Time passed. A year, two years. Ten years. Fifteen years. Thirty. Ella lived contentedly. Not happily, as nobody can live a life of perfect happiness with no sorrow, but she was satisfied with her life. It was infinitely worth living.

The Underground was shut down for good. The population moved back to the surface, settling back into their old abandoned homes, saying hello to long-lost friends. They moved far and wide; for the first few years Ella stayed with Joe and Catherine in the city, loving every second of her new existence. With time and population growth, people started leaving for other countries, new cities. She followed them to Paris, as per her long-suppressed dream, and lived there for the rest of her life in gratitude for what she had.

New governments formed worldwide. Megan Masters became the head of one, and she led a very successful and wealthy nation. Vicky White became the head of another, and earned international acclaim for her diplomatic leadership style. Life flourished and thrived on the surface since the scientists came up with innovative ways to repair it. It took a very long time but it worked. The greenhouse gas levels went down significantly and with the forests replanted and rivers cleaned of sewage, it became a healthy and beautiful place to live. The weather slowly but surely calmed and Thickair eventually disappeared entirely. Finally, you could go outside and breathe clean, fresh air, without worry of being poisoned by it. Just like the old days her mother remembered.

Her friends visited often from their new homes all across the world. Her father joined her in Paris after a few years and they lived close to each other. They went for a weekly coffee chat at a local café and wandered the river Seine in the twilight with the Eiffel Tower sparkling in the distance. That was one of her favourite things to draw.

One day she found an old drawing. The one she had done that day she realised she wanted to live here. She'd forgotten the two friends she'd drawn. They looked exactly like Lacey and Matt in a photograph they'd taken on one of their visits to see her. She stared at the pencil lines, smiling.

It was easy to forget that were was hope in those dark days. She had often thought about the Underground in the many years since she'd left it and it always seemed gloomy and cold. But there had been chinks of light in the darkness, too small for her to see at the time, and she cherished them more than anything now. She had felt like nothing there, insignificant, but there were people who cared about her and looked after her then. She just had to open her eyes to her potential. To her happiness.

And that, truly, had been worth seeking...

THE END